About the Author

Harriet Young is based in Cheshire and lives with her husband and cats.

After studying law at the University of Manchester and deciding there was no way on earth she would ever be a lawyer, Harriet worked in various jobs before retraining as a primary school teacher in 2016, where she loved teaching young children to read and share her passion for books. Harriet is now a content creation specialist, and spends her days writing and creating imagery.

Harriet has an ardent interest in history, and prefers to read and write books with an historical grounding. Mainly a thriller writer, Harriet's books are gripping, tense and sometimes terrifying. She loves to write about those times in history when the horrifying has happened – events you can't believe actually took place.

As well as writing, Harriet loves photography and reading, and combines the two on her Instagram account: @thesenovelthoughts

The Hellion

The Hellion

Harriet Young

unbound

This edition first published in 2021

Unbound
TC Group, Level 1, Devonshire House, One Mayfair Place
London W1J 8AJ

www.unbound.com
All rights reserved

ISBN (eBook): 978-1-78352-920-9
ISBN (Paperback): 978-1-78352-921-6

Cover design by Mecob

Printed and bound in Great Britain by Clays Ltd, Elcograf S.p.A.

For Michael

Super Patrons

ADW Decorators (Lancaster)
Saika Ahmed
Ceyrone Akkawi
Julia Arrington
Adam Ball
Zara Barnfield
Jason Bartholomew
John Bedi
Jessica Behegan
Heather Blanchard
Rebecca Blockley
Annabelle Blythe
Jacob Blythe
Richard Blythe
Stephanie Blythe
Alison Bolton

Elizabeth Bradley
Madison Brinker
Kelli Bryan
Joseph Burne
Reilly Campbell
Sandra Carvalho
Kelsie Christensen
Ann Clough
Beverley Ann Clough
Robyn Cooke
Sophie Cooke
Susan Cooke
Lianne Cooper
Robert Cox
Coral Davies
Stephanie Dawson
Rachel Deary
Laura Driscoll
Lauren Du Bignon
Marijn Duits
Lee Edwards
Shane Evans
Catherine Ewart
David Fairer
Paco Flores-Kiejda

Beate Friedrich
Michael Friedrich
Xiana Fumega Domínguez
Helen Gambarota
Lana Garrett
Paddy Gill
Ellie Goddard
Aymara González Montoto
Alex Green
James Grime
Professor Phil Harris
Helen and Mike
George Hughes
Andrew Hurley
Berni Hurton
Gail Jones
Andrew Khan
Malcolm Khan
Rachael Kinsella
Emma Knowles
Céline Külling
Pete Langman
Alan Lewis
Jessica Luker
Pat Luker

Catherine Rose Maw

Helen Maw

Christian & Aisha McAleenan

Mark McCabe

Tom McGuirk

Felix Mclaughlin

Jason Mclaughlin

Nicole Medin

Morgan Mills

Jamie Moans

Fran Mulhern

Abby Mulvaney

Laura Murdoch

Jessica Neumann

Sandra Newton

Alison Nichols

Mark O'Connor

Caoimhe O'Gorman

Penny Orthmann

Becky Owen

Doriane Pittet

Jonathan Potter

Janet Rawlings

Rebecca Read

Ashley Redwine

Alexandra Richiteanu

Calum Roberts

Holly Roberts

Laura Robin

Angeles Sanchez

Sharon Sawyers

Abbi Shaw

Laura Silva

Liz Smith

Hannah Spencer

Ioana Stanculescu

Elizabeth Standring

Romey Sylvester

Jennifer TenEyck

Penelope Thomas

Victoria Thornton

Adam Tinworth

Alexandra Toller

Chris and Alex Toller

Florence Toller

Henry Toller

Víctor Toller

Liz Toller-Blackburn

Jane Turnbull Lyon

Aileen Ugalde

Abbie Ward
Isabella Rae Wharton-Mclellan
Megan White
Michael Williams
Alice Young
David Young
Koala Young
Michael Young
Panda Young
Tricia Young
Wikje Zelisse

This is a fictionalised account of the lives of some of those accused of witchcraft during the 1612 Pendle witch trials.

Detailed information about these women and men is scarce.

'When it comes to the past, everyone writes fiction.'

— Stephen King

Prologue

With a crack, the cradle is empty
   The mother is sobbing
   The cradle is empty
   With a crack

The sun never shone down by Malkin Tower. That's what everyone said. The place was brown, or grey in the winter, and enveloped in a smell – the smell of death, someone told me. There'd be children about, dirty ones wearing rags, you'd never go past that way if you could help it because they'd rob you. But the kids weren't the worst thing, even if they were lice-ridden. No. The worst thing was those evil demons, witches – murderers, the lot of them. Some in my family met a sticky end at the hands of them, and there's a dozen families in the valley who could say the same thing.

Even now, even now after the whole place is gone, razed to the ground after the trial, I wouldn't go down that way. I'd rather walk a hundred miles out of my way. Why? Well. They really tried their best to get them, and they got most, and I do feel better for that. But the worst one. The worst one by far. She survived. And I know she did some terrible, terrible things. I saw her. She did them to me, she did them to my family, she even did them to her own heathen kind. And she's out there still. I'm always looking over my shoulder.

Sometimes my grandchildren will say to me, 'Why you thinking about that, Ma, it's been years and she were just a child, what harm could she do?' And I'll say, 'You just count yourselves lucky you didn't have to live it, if you had you'd know.' I'm not misremembering, even if I am getting on in years a bit now, because others know it too. I'm not being superstitious, because others know it too. No one goes down that way, by Malkin Tower. She could be anywhere, that one, and if she decided she wanted to get revenge against one of us, well, we wouldn't have a chance. Keep yourself to yourself, that's my advice, don't go near that evil ruin. And for what it's worth, make sure you say your prayers. Although they didn't help us much back then.

1

With thundering hooves
   The fall; an instant, an eternity
   A skull cracked like an egg
   Like an egg

1537 WHALLEY, LANCASHIRE

They were collecting sticks for the fire when they saw it. It was a cold day for June, and it would be a cold night.

'Annie, look!' Elizabeth gasped, pointing towards the horizon.

They had reached the crest of a small hill and, following the line of Elizabeth's arm, Anne could see in the distance smoke billowing towards the iron-grey sky. She dropped her armful of sticks.

'It's the abbey!' she yelled and set off running down the hill, calling Elizabeth to follow her.

'Stop, Annie!' Elizabeth threw her own sticks aside and raced after her. Fire was never a good thing, not that much fire anyway. She ran and ran, jumping over tree roots and low, stone walls to try to catch her friend. Anne was always the faster runner; she was only seven and could beat most of the boys in the village, so Elizabeth didn't have much of a chance. Before long though, Elizabeth saw Anne stop dead in the middle of a field. The view to the abbey here was very clear, and when Elizabeth caught her, clutching her side and gasping for breath, she saw what had halted Anne so suddenly. Men on horses. Men in armour on horses, looking like metal giants breathing fire. The girls were still a fair way away, but even so the smell of the raging furnace hit them with fury.

'Annie...' Elizabeth whispered, grasping her hand.

Anne stood still as a mountain, and did not turn to face her friend. A tear carved its way down her cheek. A breeze suddenly whipped up and her tangled blonde hair blew over her face, but she made no effort to sweep it away from her eyes.

Elizabeth knew exactly why. Smoke and fire

were pouring from the abbey grounds, but the imposing abbey was made almost entirely from stone. The buildings that were much more likely to be burning were the wooden outbuildings, and Anne's father worked in the stables. Elizabeth's mother sometimes cleaned in the abbey, a favour from the abbot, but because the building was so sturdy she wasn't afraid for her.

From this distance, Elizabeth could see glints of metal – the men were drawing their swords – and she pulled Anne with all her might over to a crumbling stone wall on the edge of the field. When they were hidden, Anne shook Elizabeth's arms away, crouched down and hid her face in her hands. Elizabeth knelt next to her, closed her eyes and waited.

When she had been younger, she didn't know how old, Elizabeth's father had been arrested. She could remember now the men on horses who had arrived at their home, the thud of their hooves on the mud path. Her mother's face had gone ashen at the sound, and she had hidden Elizabeth under a pile of rags in the corner. The men dismounted with a jangle of iron on iron and thumped on the door. Her mother had glanced desperately at Elizabeth's hiding place, pressed her fingers to her lips, then opened the door. Through a small gap in the rags, trying desperately not to move or breathe, Elizabeth could see the men silhouetted against the doorframe, huge with their helmets and cloaks. One of the men had thrown her mother to the ground and she had stayed there. Her father had been sitting on a stool by the fire, mending his boots. He did not stand when his wife hit the floor, but carried on with his needle and thread, humming slightly. Two of the men had swept into the room – the scent of smoke and leather filled Elizabeth's nostrils – grabbed her father under the armpits and dragged him away without a sound. That was the last time she saw him (although she hadn't seen much of him before then either) and her mother eventually explained to her that he'd been hanged three weeks later. For stealing a sheep.

Lots of children grew up without a ma or a pa, that was just the way things were. Some went away, for a job, and never came back. Many died. There were often outbreaks and although the young children and old ones were usually the ones to go, sometimes a strong adult would pass. So Elizabeth never felt sad about having no pa, apart from when the Nutter children from the farm across the way yelled at her, but it had been their sheep her father had stolen after all.

Still, she knew why Anne was so sad. Her ma was already gone, childbirth; she lived with her pa and her grandma and there were five other children, the littlest one only crawling, so who would keep their family going now? When the abbot was back, he would probably help, like he'd helped Ma after Pa was taken away. The abbot said the Bible teaches everyone to be charitable to those in need.

When some time had passed, more sounds came from the abbey – clanking and shouting. Elizabeth dared to peer over the wall. As far as she could see, the men were getting ready to leave. They were hurling sacks over their horses, and yelling to one another. Eventually, they were all ready and the horses began to canter away in a cloud of dust. They came perilously close to Anne and Elizabeth, who ducked beneath their wall and tried not to look at the grey, dusty giants hurtling down the path, stinking of scorched flesh and sweat. Fortunately, the men were distracted, cheerful, and did not spot the two small girls.

'Annie, let's go,' Elizabeth hissed when the men were a safe distance away, pulling at Anne's arm.

Anne gazed up at her with eyes dark and bruised from crying. She allowed Elizabeth to pull her along silently, and together they trod carefully over the ever more singed grass towards the abbey. Elizabeth had been right – the abbey still stood, but there were no welcoming candles flickering in the windows. The building was dark, ominous.

They walked apprehensively through the stone gate and around the northernmost abbey wall towards the stables. As soon as they had passed the wall, Elizabeth bent double and, gasping, vomited onto the floor.

Elizabeth's mother lay there, glazed eyes staring at the heavens, her brown dress pulled up over her hips exposing a gaping wound to her stomach. White, icy still. There was no way anyone could survive an incision like that. Elizabeth crawled over to her, shock causing her to shake, put her arms around her mother's neck and began to sob into her shoulder.

Anne swallowed back bile and left her friend with her mother's corpse. She slowly walked towards the raging furnace, which used to be a stable, eyes fixed in front of her.

'Child?' a disembodied voice whispered.

Anne whipped around to see a monk hiding behind a pile of barrels, his round face sweating from the otherworldly heat.

'Have they gone?'

Anne nodded, her lips tightly shut, and kept

walking towards the stable. There was an echoing, creaking noise and with a crash, part of the roof fell away. Anne lifted her head – she had hit the ground – and saw that the monk had pulled her safely from a falling, burning beam which now lay smouldering on the floor beside her.

'Don't go any further!' the monk spluttered, his red face smeared with ash. 'They came and created Hell, and now Hell is here on earth! God forgive me, I could not save them!'

'Who?' Anne asked tremulously. 'Where is everyone?'

The monk simply closed his eyes and muttered prayers under his breath, rocking back and forth towards the ground.

Anne knew she shouldn't be surprised about this. The king's men had come weeks before to arrest the abbot. Pa had said that they didn't like the old religion any more, they had to do something different now, but the abbot had carried on. All the people in Whalley still went to the abbey, they still sprinkled salt over the graves of the dead to keep away the evil, and Abbot Paslew still said the last rites and lit the incense and said the secret, precious prayers. Pa said this was wrong now, they had to do things the new way and the king must have heard. Anne didn't know what the new way was. Whatever this was, it must be the new way. It must be what they had to do.

'My pa works in the stables. I need to go and help him.'

The monk grabbed her arm, fingernails dug into her flesh. Anne twisted her arm, desperately trying to free herself.

'Look. Look at it!' He gestured towards the stable, the glow hurt Anne's eyes. 'Nobody was left alive.'

Still Anne struggled to free her arm, numb to the words he said to her. He clung on, red eyes burning into hers, until she felt pure exhaustion wash over her and she fell limp.

The monk turned away from Anne towards the abbey wall. Still muttering and murmuring his forbidden prayers, he raised his arms towards something on the wall, something thrust through a window on a spike and left for the world to see. It was wrapped in chains, skeletal, with rags hanging from arms and gangling, loose legs. Its face, if it could still be called that, tipped sideways from a broken, purple neck, mouth gaping wide and eyes blank.

The sky tipped inwards. Time stopped.

'Who is it?' Anne asked the monk, who raised

his head towards the sky and muttered, as though he wished it were untrue.

'The abbot. The king has returned him.'

2

Abnormal character
   Aberrant, monstrous
   Anomalous phenomenon
   Inconceivable, macabre

1549 – WHALLEY, LANCASHIRE

Elizabeth had slowed to a dawdle, deeply breathing in the crisp air. It was approaching her least favourite time of year, when life faded away and there was nothing left but the howling, biting wind. But despite this, the changing of the seasons always filled her with a strange excitement and restlessness. This was the first truly cold day of the year. She felt the icy touch cleansing her, shaking away the last dust of summer.

Anne's grandmother, Old Eaprick, would be cross that she was taking her time, but she had long known that the woman's bark was worse than her bite. She was a caring woman at heart, and she had certainly shown charity when she took not only Anne and her siblings into her home after they were orphaned, but Elizabeth too.

It had been Elizabeth's turn to go to market, to pick up the various bits and pieces Old Eaprick needed for her work. It was always an odd collection – bottles of the most specific size one day, rabbit hearts the next. Today, it was orange balm and nutmeg. Fortunately the vendors knew Old Eaprick well, and they always got a good price.

The path was well trodden, but there were few people around today. Despite it being market day, the milling festival had taken place yesterday and those who were around looked worn out.

Elizabeth could see just one shadow ahead of her, some distance away and walking in the same direction. The person was likely a customer of Old Eaprick, and as they approached the cottage Elizabeth was proved right. The person – Elizabeth could make out now that it was a man – entered the cottage about a minute before she did.

'Good,' Old Eaprick said as Elizabeth opened the door, 'I need those now.'

The main room in the cottage was dominated by an enormous fireplace, adorned with bottles and bowls of herbs and spices, dried grasses and berries, and pelts and skins. There was a stool near the fire, where customers usually sat, and on the stool sat the man, his back to the door.

Anne was asking him the questions. This was Anne's job. They had taken it in turns to start with, but Anne was better at it.

'What is the trouble?' Anne asked the man in a honeyed voice. She caught Elizabeth's eye behind the man's back and grinned.

'My brother is ill.'

Another smirk from Anne, hidden quickly. There was always a brother or a sister or an aunt, never the person themselves.

Old Eaprick cleared her throat gently, and Elizabeth hastened over to the work bench, depositing her parcel on it. Old Eaprick would listen to Anne's conversation, and by the time the talk was finished the treatment would be ready. Sometimes it was simple – if a woman needed help with a birth, for example, she would be sent on her way with a medicine of peppermint and willow bark to help with discomfort, and a promise that when the time came, she would be there.

Sometimes it was more difficult – a neighbourly dispute, or a matrimonial quarrel.

Elizabeth quietly opened the parcel and began preparing the ingredients for storage, passing Old Eaprick a small amount of each for her tincture. Old Eaprick's busy hands worked deftly, chopping, crushing, burning. Her work was intuitive, she worked by touch now that her eyes had started to fail.

'A cough that won't go,' the man was saying.

'How long?' Anne was close to him, the conversation intimate. This was part of her skill. She had placed a soothing hand on his knee and he had leaned in towards her, disclosing his problems.

'This whole summer.'

'Is he bed-bound?'

The man shook his head, keeping contact with Anne's soothing eyes. 'But he can't do the work he used to. He's getting weaker.'

Anne nodded, gripping his knee tighter with her hand. 'You must be very worried.'

Elizabeth was captivated, she always was. When Elizabeth and Anne had first been given the job of talking to the clients, they had been sneering of it, hadn't seen it as a real skill. But Anne had something special. When Elizabeth used to talk, she felt their eyes slip over to Anne – they were aware of the room, they were restless. Anne brought about a trance. She was hypnotic.

Before long, the cough syrup was ready and, in a smooth movement, Old Eaprick passed it to Anne who pressed it into the man's hand, before wrapping the hand in both of hers. The man blinked, several times, shaken out of his reverie and stood. He looked around the room for the first time and seemed surprised to see Elizabeth and Old Eaprick there. He smiled at them both. Elizabeth smiled back wryly, and Anne led him outside where she would discuss payment.

The rest of the week was busy; there was a sickness which afflicted many of the townsfolk, and Old Eaprick ran out of ginger by Friday. Elizabeth was sent into town to find more, and it was there that she bumped into the man, quite literally.

'You're from Old Eaprick's?' he asked, gently holding the tops of her arms to stop her from tumbling after the collision.

'Yes. Sorry.' Elizabeth collected herself and picked up her ginger from the muddy path. The man helped her, brushing the majority of the mud from each piece.

'Robert,' he said, handing the ginger to her.

Elizabeth was momentarily confused, before realising that he was telling her his name. 'Elizabeth.'

Robert looked down at her, smiling. He was at least a head taller than her, and had a nice, roughly weathered face. There were crinkles at the eyes, which glittered out with bright whiteness. Elizabeth guessed that he was perhaps ten years old than her, and he had the muscled physique of a well-fed farmer.

'I'll walk you back to the cottage, if I can. I have need of Old Eaprick's services again.'

Elizabeth consented; he seemed entirely harmless. The walk was short, and they spent it with light, meaningless talk. Sometimes in life, you didn't realise that the best times were happening until they were gone. In the future, Elizabeth would come to look back on this walk as a fleeting moment of true happiness. Although they spoke of nothing, really, Robert was kind and easy and laughed often.

'Tell me what it's like living there,' Robert gestured towards the cottage as they approached it.

'I've hardly known anything else.'

'That doesn't answer the question.'

Elizabeth paused and thought carefully for a moment. 'Old Eaprick is kind. She teaches us. In ten years she says I'll know everything I need to know, and then when she dies I can take her place.'

'What about Annie?'

'Oh, Annie too.'

Robert furrowed his brow. 'Is that what you want?'

Elizabeth laughed lightly. 'Well, what else would I do? I have no family. I'm too old to start learning another job. Who wants a nineteen-year-old chambermaid?'

Robert didn't reply. They had reached the door of the cottage, and Elizabeth gestured him inside in front of her.

'Robert has need of our services again!' Elizabeth called to Old Eaprick and Anne, who both turned with a matching odd look at the sound of her loud, clear voice. Elizabeth bowed her head, made her way over to the bench and allowed Anne to lead Robert to the stool.

'What do you think of Robert?' Anne asked. It was evening, and they were tidying the cottage before going to bed.

Elizabeth looked at her in surprise. 'Why?'

A smirk appeared on Anne's face. She twirled a curl of her blonde hair around a finger.

'I think he wants to marry me!'

Elizabeth laughed, but stopped suddenly when she saw that Anne wasn't playing.

'But, Annie…'

'What? I think he's quite handsome, don't you?'

'I suppose…'

'And he has land, he said. And what else am I supposed to do?'

'What do you mean?'

'I mean, do you plan to stay here for your whole life? In this cottage? No children, no adventure?'

Elizabeth thought back to the conversation with Robert that very morning. Of course, that's what he'd been asking. About Anne. And now he planned to take her best friend, her only comfort, away from her.

'Annie. We'll be happy here. We can earn our own money. We'll be respected.'

'Respected or feared? Haven't you noticed how people look at us? Like we're not normal. I want to get away from it, Elizabeth. Surely you understand? A man is the way out. A man is the path to security, a normal family.'

Elizabeth was silent for a while. This was the first time Anne had ever said anything like this. But now that she thought about it, it was true. Robert was the first outsider who had ever been easy with her, and it had been so nice.

'I understand,' she said heavily. 'But what am I to do?'

Anne said nothing, and put her hand over Elizabeth's. It was clear to see what Anne thought. A man was an easy escape for beautiful Anne. What would Elizabeth do?

Over the next few weeks, Robert carried on visiting the cottage and it seemed as though everything Anne had said was coming to fruition. He would arrive with three late roses, one for each of them, and would stay to talk long after his tincture was ready.

Anne and Elizabeth didn't discuss him again but their conversation remained heavy in the air. Something had broken between them. Elizabeth felt a loss, like grief, as she mourned her future life with Anne. Anne, stubborn as ever, refused to notice.

Old Eaprick watched all of this and muttered to herself, glaring at Robert and throwing his offerings of roses on the fire. Elizabeth took this to mean that the old woman agreed with her, but no words were exchanged.

On the evening of the Monday of the fourth week of Robert's visits, Elizabeth was collecting berries alone in the waning light when she heard the breaking of twigs underfoot behind her.

She froze, senses heightened, began to turn slowly and was so shocked that she screamed when hands gripped her sides from behind.

'Got you!' Robert laughed, all mirthful eyes and bright glimpses of teeth.

'What are you doing here?' Hand on her heart, she willed the uncomfortable thrumming to slow.

'Looking for you, of course.'

He looked odd, his eyes were too intense, his cheeks flushed.

'Why?' Scenarios ran through Elizabeth's mind – something had happened to Annie or Old Eaprick.

'Why? Because I wanted to see you.'

'What for?'

'Elizabeth, are you really so blind? Why do you think I've been visiting all of this time?'

Elizabeth shook her head, the realisation slowly dawning on her. She allowed herself a single, dazzling smile at Robert before another, heavier emotion hit her. Guilt.

She hadn't wanted to admit it to herself before, but part of the reason she had felt betrayed by Anne was because, once she had given it thought, she had realised that she wanted freedom too. She wanted to escape, and she had been jealous of Anne's option. Which was now her option.

'What about Annie?' The words dropped like stones.

Robert took both of her hands. 'Annie doesn't matter.'

Guilt rose again. Anne did matter. Anne was her only friend. Anne's family had taken her in when she had no one. She was everything to her.

But then, Anne had wanted to leave her alone – she wouldn't have given it another thought. And Anne was the captivating one; she would have many more options, if she wanted them. She surely wouldn't mind; this could be Elizabeth's only chance.

Before she could think any further, Robert's lips were on hers. The shock of it stilled her, and she breathed in the warm scent of him. Her insides turned molten. It felt better than she had ever imagined, enveloped in his big arms.

His hands began to move, up and down her body. She gently pushed him away.

'Not here. Not now.'

Robert groaned. 'Soon?'

'Soon.'

Elizabeth returned to the cottage with a secret smile on her face. Despite Anne's demands, she wouldn't share.

It was only two months later when, after many more visits from Robert, Elizabeth realised that her monthly bleed was late and she knew she had to tell Anne. Robert had been so good about it; he had asked for her hand immediately and told her how excited he was to marry her, as soon as possible. So it was with a light heart that Elizabeth sat down to dinner with Anne and Old Eaprick.

'I have something to tell you both,' she said, laying down her knife.

Anne and Old Eaprick looked up: Anne with eyes wide and questioning, Old Eaprick with narrow slits.

'I want to thank you both for everything you've done for me. I would be dead without you. Annie, you have been a true friend all of my life, and

Old Eaprick, you are my family now. I'm going to be sad to go, but—'

Elizabeth stopped at a loud clatter – Anne had dropped her knife on the stone flags. She left it there. She stared at Elizabeth.

'Robert and I are to marry,' Elizabeth finished.

The silence was heavy. Elizabeth looked from Old Eaprick to Anne and back again, and saw the same blank expression on each face.

'It will happen soon,' Elizabeth said, eager to break the silence, 'we are—'

'You are pregnant,' Old Eaprick said.

'Well…'

'This blood will stale.' Old Eaprick picked up her knife and continued eating, as though nothing had happened.

Anne's face was unreadable. No anger, no malice, but no happiness either. Elizabeth questioned her with her eyes, but got no response. Eventually, Anne retrieved her knife and carried on eating, without saying a word.

The day when they were to marry, just three days later, Elizabeth dressed carefully in the new dress she had made. Old Eaprick had been kind enough to buy new cloth for the dress, and Anne had helped her to make it. There had been no anger from either of the women, and Elizabeth was happy to be leaving the cottage on good terms. Yes, Anne had been extremely quiet and, yes, Old Eaprick had said those strange words, but other than that they had been almost supportive.

If she was honest with herself, Elizabeth had been expecting more of a reaction from Anne. She knew that Robert had shown her attention too, and been friendly. But Anne had taken it so well. It looked like their friendship would survive.

Still, neither Anne nor Old Eaprick took her to the church. She had pleaded with them, but they gently and firmly refused. Elizabeth was confused by this, but buried her feelings of worry. Anne gave her a little bunch of snowdrops though and Elizabeth clutched them as nerves gripped her on the short walk, her small parcel of belongings over her shoulder.

They had arranged to marry in Whalley, then they would travel to Robert's hometown of Pendle. He had been in Whalley for work, but he owned a house in Pendle: the perfect set-up for a family. They would be the most wonderful family. She was nervous about seeing the house for the first time, nervous about moving somewhere she had never been before. But Robert had been quite sure that there was no need, they would be so happy.

The church looked pretty in the January light. It was early, so that they could get the marriage done and get to Pendle before the light faded. Robert was waiting outside the church; Elizabeth recognised his broad-shouldered silhouette and picked up her pace. He waved, grinned and, when she arrived, picked her up and swung her around.

'My wife.' He smiled.

She smiled back and they walked hand in hand into the church.

The church was empty – almost. The grey, tired-looking priest was there, clutching his beads, a dusty Bible in front of him. In the pews sat two men, only one of whom turned around as they entered. These must be the witnesses that Robert had arranged. The one who turned around offered Elizabeth a small smile, before casting his eyes down towards her belly. Instinctively, Elizabeth held the snowdrops tightly over her stomach, embarrassed.

This was not the wedding Elizabeth had ever thought of, quiet and alone, the joy only hers and Robert's. It was dusty and dark, and the omens felt wrong.

3

A woman and a man
  Tied in matrimony
  Battling always
  One will end the other
  The end will come

The pot was empty, as it always was, and the children were screaming, like they always were. Elizabeth sighed and closed her tired eyes, pushed her fists into her ears and drowned out the wailing, shrieking brats. It was hard to believe she was already heavy with her seventh child. There had been six little ones (two still alive, praise God, she supposed) and another on the way. The last one; she felt it in her bones. And thank the Lord for that. Robert was a labourer, he did what he could for the family, but the work came in fits and starts and often Robert spent what he had on ale before food.

Robert's thick, dark hair had mostly disappeared in a few short years and his once straight nose had been broken a few too many times in fights after a night of ale. His eyes had been kind when they married, his eyebrows had softened when he looked at her, but she rarely got a look any more, and certainly not a kind one. Kindness had been beaten out of him by ten years of grief, loss and menial labour.

Robert and Elizabeth had moved into Robert's old mother's house that day. Elizabeth had initially assumed, when she met Robert, that he owned a house of his own. That was certainly what he had told her. While that was technically true in law, it was entirely incorrect in reality. When Robert's father had died the property had passed to him, but like any good son Robert allowed his mother to carry on living in the family home. This was all perfectly reasonable, but Elizabeth soon came to realise she had made a fatal error.

They moved in with that old bitch down at Malkin Tower in Pendle the day of the wedding and Elizabeth had become Elizabeth Southern. Elizabeth had never heard of Malkin Tower beforehand, being at least a ten-hour walk away in Whalley, but she soon learned that its name, Malkin – slut, slattern, however you wanted to say it – came about from her new mother-in-law. She had thirteen children altogether, but never married. Robert was the youngest surviving, and by the time Elizabeth moved into the building she was a foul-mouthed, seventy-year-old crone. Her hips gone, she relied on Robert for everything and demanded the same support from his new bride and subsequent grandchildren. Elizabeth had gone from living with Annie's grandma, a respected, though sometimes suspect, wise woman, to the home of a lazy sloven.

The house sat at the bottom of a hill, sheltered from the rain but not the howling wind. It was set a little way outside the nearest village, which was situated on a small rise round the other side of the hill. Robert did as he could, sometimes, to keep the house in some state of repair but it always seemed as though the ground was trying to reclaim it. Any big storm, and part of the poorly thatched, patched-up roof would fall away. Although the rain didn't often catch the house, it ran straight down the hill causing deep rivets full of mud to pour either side of the property, which Elizabeth had to wade through to get in and out.

The garden had long been abandoned when Elizabeth moved in: a tangle of weeds and thorns. Over the first few years, she had tried to tackle the patch of ground. She had grand plans of growing a few herbs and using all of those skills she'd learned from Annie's grandmother, but try as she might the ground would not clear – creepers returned, nettles and thorns covered the patch and climbed up the walls of the house, clawing it back into the hill. Clawing it back down to Hell, Elizabeth sometimes thought.

Elizabeth could still vividly remember the moment she had seen the property. Walking down the hill on the path, holding Robert's hand after their nuptials, a heavy, happily tired feeling enveloping her from the walk.

'Just around this corner now,' Robert had murmured, looking apprehensive beneath his weathered brow, which was just beginning to furrow.

Elizabeth had smiled at him cheerfully, confident in her youth and her beauty and her luck, which had led her to this moment: the start of her new life with her husband and child.

The sun had been shining on that day, but as

the path led around the side of the hill against which Malkin Tower was nestled, a thick, heavy rain cloud moved in front of the sun and the day turned suddenly cold and dark. Malkin Tower slowly but surely came into view and an uncomfortable feeling began to embed itself in the pit of Elizabeth's stomach. She was used to poverty, she had never had money, but this place was beyond that.

Robert had firmly ensured that his eyes did not meet hers as they walked towards the house. She had glanced quickly, desperately and repeatedly up at him, horrified at the sight but too timid and nervous of her new husband to ask the question racing around her head: *Surely that's not it?*

Closer to the house, fifty yards away, the stench hit her. Dead and rotting meat, faeces, God only knew what caused it. Or maybe He didn't; this place looked closer to Hell. She never fully rid the place of its smell, it was embedded, part of the house, like a carving in a pew.

Still Robert had avoided her eyes. They crossed the threshold – Elizabeth assumed it was such, but the gate and fence had long since disintegrated. Elizabeth stopped and stared at the crumbling pile and Robert grabbed her hand. He had finally looked at her and his eyes had been void of passion, or love, or kindness: they were empty, resigned.

'Come on,' he had ordered grimly, pulling her forward.

Elizabeth, thinking of nothing but the neat cottage she had lived in with Annie's family, with the ordered garden and the fresh smell of herbs, was led blindly inside. Her eyes took a while to become accustomed to the gloom and she was very aware of herself standing there with her clean, yellow dress, her dark hair carefully plaited and her slender right hand grasping her wilted and bruised wedding bouquet of snowdrops as though it were a lifeline – a juxtaposition to the grime.

'Is this the whore?'

The first words Robert's mother had ever spoken of her. A shadow arose in the darkness. Elizabeth began to make out a hearth – unlit, cold – and a chair.

Robert had bowed his head. Embarrassment? Fear? Resignation?

'This is Elizabeth,' he had replied.

The old woman walked unsteadily forward, right up to Elizabeth. Although a foot taller, Elizabeth recoiled from the filthy, ashen-faced skeleton. The woman spat on the floor, right at Elizabeth's feet, before turning her back and shuffling back to her chair.

Things hadn't got much better. Although Elizabeth had become stronger, thicker skinned, as the years passed, living with that woman was still a torture. Better than on the streets though, Elizabeth supposed. She was surely dying now anyway – the mother-in-law – and every kick in the womb for her new child was a kick in the chest for the dying woman.

Elizabeth's work never stopped: cleaning, washing, cooking, sewing, anything else to bring a bit of money in, even begging sometimes, so at night while she lay at rest, she placed her hands on her growing belly. Every flutter, she knew, she felt, was a flutter in the old woman's heart. And when she said her prayers at night, the old ones, the ones the abbot had taught her, she asked God that this would happen. And she knew it would. Old Eaprick had taught her all she needed to know about seventh children. This child's strength would suck the life force from the old hag, of that she was sure. They had the power of God, or the power of the Devil.

Elizabeth had used the old, forbidden magic in a fit of rage one day early in the year. It had been a frosty day in March; the ground was hard as a bone and sent a devilish chill through the bottom of your boots, particularly if they were old and full of holes, like Elizabeth's were. The previous night, she had hidden a bag of grain in the yard: she buried it by the wall. She had earned it for mending some clothes for Mary North in the village and it was supposed to see them through the next few weeks. Robert hadn't found any work for an age; his reputation was poor now. He had turned up drunk too many times, and there had been petty thefts, which no one could prove were him but happened far too often when he was around. He was a last resort. The grain was their only food source, until either Elizabeth or Robert could work again. But that morning, that cold March day, Elizabeth had woken up to find the spot where she had buried the grain dishevelled; the sack wasn't there. It had been dug up.

Panicking for the children, little Christopher and Robert, she had flown back into the house to where the old woman was sitting, as always, in her chair next to the empty hearth. She was asleep, mouth open, snoring loudly. Elizabeth shook her roughly, to wake her, and as she did a dislodged bottle rolled out of the old woman's clothing onto the floor. It was empty, and as the spluttering woman awoke, Elizabeth waved it in front of her nose.

'Mead?' Elizabeth said. 'You've sold our only food for mead?'

The woman blinked, bleary-eyed, and her lips began to curl into a grin. 'I'll do as I wish,' she murmured, before closing her eyes.

Elizabeth shook her once more, but she steadfastly kept her eyes closed and refused to acknowledge any more of Elizabeth's shouts.

Elizabeth gave up and stormed back outside. Christopher and little Robert were crouching by the hole that had contained the grain, and they were crying. Her heart bled for those two little boys who had known too much hunger in their short lives. Rage began to fill Elizabeth. She felt its heat in the pit of her belly. It flew outwards; her hands shook and she felt her face grow angry, red blotches. Action was necessary.

'Come on,' she said tersely to her boys, pulling them up to standing.

Robert went out early that morning. He'd said he was going to find work, but Elizabeth knew where she would find him if he had been lucky.

She stormed, with the little boys whimpering and moaning, up the hill and round the side. It was a twenty-minute walk to the village, and the boys didn't have much energy. Elizabeth wished she hadn't had to bring them out, but she could think of no other way. She couldn't leave them with the hag. Elizabeth was so filled with fury that she was spurred on; her speed was high. Christopher, trying to keep up, tripped on the path and grazed his knee. He cast one terrified look at his mother and tried not to cry. Elizabeth saw his expression and her resolve was almost broken. But she had to keep going now. It was the only way.

She swept Christopher into her arms – though he was six, he was small and light – and kept walking. Faster, faster, faster. Robert trotted along beside them, desperate to keep up, scared to ask where they were going.

The inn was on the far edge of the village. That was where they were heading. If Robert hadn't been lucky, he would still be begging on the street and they would see him on the way. Sometimes, Elizabeth wondered how long he had been begging rather than working, drinking away their livelihood just like his mother. She had become resigned to it, to him and his mother, but this was the final straw. Something had to change. This couldn't keep happening. Weak, Robert was led by his mother. No more.

The village was really nothing more than a

cluster of houses around the church. One main road cut through the centre, past the church, and it was well trodden by travellers passing through on the route between Lancaster and Leeds. There was a line of various shops, the butcher, the blacksmith, the baker, on either side of the road and behind them, down jennels between, more houses were tucked away.

Fortunately, it was quiet that day; the villagers were on the whole distrustful of Elizabeth's family, and sometimes shouted at her. The cold weather was forcing them indoors; she could smell woodsmoke on the air and felt a swift pang of jealousy about those who were so well off that they could have their fires lit all day.

They stalked through the village, their breath clouding in the cold air, looking this way and that way for Robert. He wasn't sitting outside the church, cap in hand, bothering passers-by as she had seen him doing one day recently, a sight which had filled her with burning shame and made her understand the other villagers' distrust of her. He wasn't knocking on doors, gathering the pity, repulsion or disgust of people they had to see on a daily basis. That meant only one thing, despite the early hour (unless he had found a job – unlikely though).

Elizabeth, still determined, still feeling the energising rage, put her head down and broke into a run as she approached the inn. She ignored the two children, both now starting to sob out of cold, out of fear, out of confusion.

She threw open the door to the inn and her eyes, flitting around the room, fell on Henry Slack, the innkeeper. A large, round man with greasy, thinning hair.

'Is he here?' Elizabeth asked shortly.

Henry nodded his head, briefly, once, then gestured behind him. Elizabeth walked through the room, through the door at the back, and out to the courtyard where the barrels were stored. Leaning against one of them was Robert. He raised his blood-shot eyes and frowned.

'Bess?'

'You needn't move. I need you to take the children. I have something I must do.' Elizabeth refused to meet his eyes; she found the sight of him fairly repulsive. He could only have been here for two hours, but he was already slow and bleary.

'Can't Mother have them? I might be working later.'

Elizabeth shook her head at the feeble lie. 'She

looks worse than you do. There's no food in the house. You can find them something to eat.'

'What are you doing?' Robert asked, heaving himself upwards.

There was no embarrassment about how he had been found. He didn't seem to care.

Elizabeth ignored him and unhooked Christopher's arms from around her neck. She tenderly placed him on the floor, leaning against one of the barrels. He looked up at her, his big eyes glistening. She kissed him and his brother on the top of their heads.

'I'll be back soon. Don't worry,' she muttered to them, before turning and leaving the inn without a backwards glance.

'Elizabeth! Elizabeth!'

She could hear Robert shouting. She ignored him. About time he looked after those children.

She broke into a run, down the road through the middle of the village, back the way she had come. With this speed, the cold began to feel comfortable. She was determined, set. She knew exactly what she needed to do.

After the last house in the village, there was a fork in the road. There was the path which led back to Malkin Tower, and there was the path which led up Pendle Hill. Elizabeth turned right, onto the path which led up the hill. The start of the path was well trodden, used often by farmers with their sheep, or villagers foraging. However, the further up the hill Elizabeth walked, the less obvious the path was. Woodland closed in on either side and it became dense, dark. Elizabeth felt the familiar tingling as she climbed the hill, getting gradually out of breath. The place was special. She had always known that. Annie's grandmother had brought them up here on a few occasions, when she needed to, and Elizabeth had seen what had happened. This place had power.

Close to the top of the hill, the trees began to thin out. It was inhospitable up here, nothing really grew apart from the bracken. Elizabeth quickly gathered together some short sticks which had fallen to the ground, a length of ivy and some moss. With this, she proceeded to the very top of the hill.

The peak was flat and long, and Elizabeth had to walk a little further to the right place. There was a large rock, the height of a man, about midway along the crest and that was where Elizabeth was heading. There, in the shadow of that rock, was where she would do it.

She had only witnessed Old Eaprick do this

once, but she wasn't concerned – she knew she would remember what to do and she knew it would work. Anne's grandmother had said that this was something you could do once in a lifetime, any more was bad luck, and to choose wisely. Elizabeth felt certain that this was the right choice. God couldn't be angry, not when the one she was cursing was a demon.

In the shadow of the rock, Elizabeth sat where generations of women had sat before her. The ground was icy and the wind was bitter, whistling around her and around the rock. Quickly, before her fingers turned numb from the cold, Elizabeth wound the ivy around two sticks in the shape of a cross. Then, she used more sticks and ivy to fashion legs, arms and a head. All of the time, she muttered the name, 'Agnes, Agnes, Agnes, Agnes.' The name of her mother-in-law.

When it was finished, she held it tightly in her hands, kneeling on the ground. She rocked back and forth, murmuring over and over the words and sounds she had heard Annie's grandmother murmur. She threw herself into it; she knew she had to ride the anger and the injustice and the hatred she felt. Over and over, she rocked and rocked. Part of the effigy fell away under her tight grip, but she didn't notice.

Her eyes were squeezed shut, she was rocking, rocking, murmuring. Beads of sweat grew on her forehead, and beneath her arms, but she didn't notice. She kept going, kept going until the effort and the focus and the hunger she felt caused her to lose grip of time. Still, she kept going, she kept going. Once, she opened her eyes briefly and thought she saw a huge black dog prowling near her. She closed her eyes and carried on.

Elizabeth felt cold earth beneath her head. She slowly opened her eyes. She was lying prone on the ground. It was dusk, but she didn't know if days had passed. The effigy was gone. The dog was gone. It had worked. She felt it, deep inside. A warmth, despite the chill.

She pushed her hands into the ground and heaved herself up. Her dress was soaking, she was shaking slightly. It was time to go home.

When she had managed to negotiate the path down the hill, with many trips and almost falls, she arrived back at the Tower with an unmovable sense of peace inside. Robert and the boys were there. Robert was humming as he lit the fire with a handful of dry twigs – he had a rabbit, he must have poached it – and the boys were chattering happily with anticipation for the hot food to come.

The old woman was still in her chair by the hearth, still asleep. She looked as though she hadn't moved for years. Elizabeth smiled inwardly. Soon, she wouldn't.

That night, with a belly full of rabbit and an overwhelming sense of purpose, Elizabeth took her husband in her arms and enjoyed lovemaking like she never had before. That night created a new life.

And here they were. This day, as Elizabeth walked with her children to the well, the baby was kicking particularly heavily. She left young Christopher and Robert there with the other women, having had a strong, overwhelming need to return to the house and see the woman. She found Agnes sitting by the unlit hearth – she never lit it, she seemed to prefer the damp – covered in blankets with her hands clutched to her chest.

'Dearest mother!' Elizabeth exclaimed at her distress, smiling as she felt the child kick and move. 'Are you ill?'

The old woman shook her head, grasped at her chest and spat at Elizabeth. 'Witch!' she spluttered.

A kind of loving greeting by now, Elizabeth supposed wryly. Elizabeth had tried, ever since that first day, to forge a relationship with that woman, but she was always resistant. Bitterness towards Agnes was deep in her bones.

Elizabeth stepped back away from her, then suddenly, keenly in her sides, felt the tell-tale signs of labour. The shack had only one other room, and Elizabeth didn't fancy the unending foul diatribe from that woman, or being around when the hag took what was inevitably her dying breath, and so hitched up her skirts and headed determinedly towards the door.

'Don't you dare leave this house!' the old woman gasped. Her dry, creased skin was pale and her skeletal fingers were fluttering around her throat. 'You stay here and see what you're doing to me!'

Elizabeth stopped and turned to face her.

'What I'm doing to you?' she hissed, pacing towards her mother-in-law. 'You deserve every last thing that comes to you. I hope your every breath is like daggers in your throat. I hope your insides heat and turn to molten metal, burning you from the inside out. I hope your eyes are blinded by visions of the hell you're going to!' Elizabeth stepped back, blinking and finding her breath.

The old crone had made Elizabeth's life something of a misery, that was true, but she had never dared react like this before. In that moment, though, a flood of memories of injustices and malice had rushed over her. The time when Elizabeth, exhausted and overwhelmed from giving birth to her first child hours before, had been forced out on the streets to beg so the old prostitute could entertain a client. The time that child had caught a fever from shivering in the cold for six hours, that December day, and died. The time the old bitch had laughed at her grief, drunk, and said she'd lose plenty more before her life was through. The times she had whispered poison into her son's ear, encouraging him to fly into a rage at Elizabeth or their children. The times she'd taken her son's earnings and used it for her own pleasure rather than feeding the starving bairns that lived under the same roof as her. The fact that she'd forced herself on her son's good-will, lived in the house that was rightfully his, and contributed nothing.

'Ah!' Elizabeth gasped. Another contraction. This one brought her to her knees. She gripped her sides and moaned, quickly trying to calculate. It was too soon. It must be too soon.

Old Mother Southern grinned through her own grimaces. 'Looks like your evil curse will see you off too! Ha! And I doubt I'll be meeting one of your kind at the gates.' She clutched her chest suddenly, coinciding with an all-consuming vice of pain in Elizabeth.

Christopher, Elizabeth's little boy, took this moment to come into the house. Just six years old, he'd been collecting berries on his way back from the well, which he dropped all over the floor when he saw his mother and grandmother gasping and prone in the room.

'Christopher! Go and fetch Annie!' Elizabeth gasped.

Christopher paused for a little while, his chubby face twisted with bewilderment, but with a glance from Elizabeth he fled from the house, running as fast as he could to the village, to the house that Anne shared with her daughters, Bessie (who Elizabeth liked to think was her namesake) and Anne. They had moved to Pendle after the death of Old Eaprick, when Anne herself got married, and had lived there ever since.

What seemed like hours passed. Elizabeth had crawled through to the other room, the bedroom which normally housed them all, and knelt on the floor by her bed, repeating prayer after prayer after forbidden prayer. It was too early. How much too early, she wasn't sure, it was enough to remember her own name some days, never mind count the months. But it was waning autumn now, and the child shouldn't be born until midwinter. Of that she was certain.

Every now and then, she could hear the panting gasps of her failing mother-in-law from the other room, which was separated by a thin rag curtain rather than a door. Not once would she call out to her, though. Not once would she beg for help from her, not even if her soul depended on it. She counted between the pain, as Old Eaprick had taught her when they'd helped with the births years before, but never before had she been to a birth when this much blood had gushed so early. She closed her eyes and prayed again.

What could have been days later, or minutes, she heard the welcome yelling of Anne.

'She didn't send you for that one?' Elizabeth heard her shout in disbelief to Christopher. Elizabeth imagined her gesturing at the wrinkled beast slumped by the fire. Christopher must have shaken his head, because at once, Anne stormed into the bedroom, Bessie and Anne right behind her.

'It's too soon,' she said matter-of-factly. 'You'll have to brace yourself to lose this one. But count yourself lucky.' She lowered her voice and tipped her head towards the curtain. 'Looks like that one's had it too.'

With that, Anne set to work, sending the children on missions, mostly unnecessary, while she lay Elizabeth back on the bed and did what she could to stop the bleed.

Elizabeth sweated and groaned and passed in and out of consciousness. Strange memories… helping Old Eaprick bottle herbs and spices; collecting grasses with Annie; dancing through the fields and moors with the youthful joy of being alive; her mother, thrust to the floor by a soldier; her mother, lying in a pool of blood at the abbey…

Elizabeth opened her eyes.

Anne, with a desperate look on her face, was dousing her with cold water. She saw the fluttering eyelids and said, 'oh, thank God, we thought you'd gone.'

Elizabeth raised her head slightly and saw the three children, Bessie, Anne and Christopher, mirroring Anne's concern on their faces.

'The child?' Elizabeth asked.

'Alive.' Anne replied, but the grim look on her face made Elizabeth suspect there was more to hear. 'We did what we could to save her. I don't know how long she'll last.' Anne passed the bundle she was holding to Elizabeth.

She took hold of her newborn daughter and gasped. As well as being tiny, like a feather, the child had one eye much higher than the other. The effect was gruesome, monstrous, although Elizabeth felt nothing but pity and love for the poor creature. She knew what people would say. Calling for Anne had been a risk. Elizabeth knew what her friend could do; she knew what she'd asked for.

'What did you do to save her, Annie?' Elizabeth asked. 'What does my baby owe?'

Anne sighed. 'I offered what I had to, to save you and the child. Your stupid curse – it killed your old mother-in-law, that's for sure. But now it's all gone. I saved your lives. Still, another needs to go. Did you know what you were doing?'

'I just wanted her gone,' Elizabeth replied distractedly, staring down at the infant.

This new life had sucked the life out of another. The curse had worked. But Anne, Anne with her skills and her childhood love for her, had created something else, something Elizabeth didn't understand. She had saved Elizabeth and her child. There must have been rules which Elizabeth didn't understand. Often, she felt slow and stupid, like she couldn't quite follow the intricacies of the world. She'd felt like this ever since she lived with Anne and her grandmother.

'A life for a life. It's your choice now. Choose your husband, or one of your children, Christopher or little Robert. One has to go,' Anne explained.

Elizabeth stared blankly at Anne's determined face. This must be wrong. Elizabeth thought she knew all about deals, she'd learned about their mysterious ways from Old Eaprick, but she'd never instigated a curse before. Surely they couldn't happen without the knowledge of the person placing the curse? A glance at Anne's face told her otherwise.

'I can't choose this one?' Elizabeth asked, gesturing at the helpless being in her arms.

'Of course not!' snapped Anne. 'You've done all this for her!'

'And the bitch is definitely dead?' Elizabeth asked, her eyes now fixed on the quietly sleeping babe.

'Yes.'

Silence. To others, it might seem strange to make this decision, to accept it. But not to Elizabeth. Everything had a cost. By calling Anne here, she had taken a risk, and Anne in her wisdom had saved who she had been asked to save. But there was always a cost. However hard that cost was.

'Then I can't choose Robert. Without him we'd starve, however hopeless he can be. Christopher is strong and healthy. Baby Robert… such hope. Such promise. He's only three.' Elizabeth trailed off, staring sadly at the girl.

'You must choose. Or the Devil will choose himself.' Anne's resolve was strong, she'd seen enough death not to be cowed by it.

'I can't choose. I won't choose. This isn't what I wished for.' Empty words. She knew she would have to.

Anne's mouth tightened into a thin line. She was the wise woman, now her grandma was gone. She was teaching her daughters the same skills. She was not used to people shrugging off her advice.

'You know this is dangerous, Elizabeth? You don't choose, the choice will still be made?'

Elizabeth raised her heavy eyes. She had made her decision, but she couldn't say it. She wouldn't say it. But God would know. Still exhausted, still weak from loss of blood, she replied, 'I don't choose. I don't believe the choice will be made. God will bless my seventh child, but I thank you for saving my life. Christopher, go and find Da. If he's at the tavern, bring him home. His mother's dead.'

Christopher blinked twice before obediently heading from the room.

'Where is baby Robert?' Anne asked gently.

Elizabeth closed her eyes. She remembered noise and fuss. 'He was with me by the well. One of the women must have him.' She lay back on her bed and gave way to exhaustion. She had been at the well just before she had had that overwhelming need to come back to the Tower and see her mother-in-law. The women in the village looked after one another's children interchangeably, and the well was close by. No need to worry.

Anne leaned back in her chair and smiled tightly. 'Girls. Find baby Robert. And Pa Robert too. You can't ignore the rules. You can't ignore God.'

4

Crushing and breaking
  Grinding and grating
  The babe will mewl
  and the scream will come

1575

Everyone avoided Malkin Tower, and why wouldn't they? The place was seething with vermin, a filthy heap. Elizabeth, already stoop-backed and shadowy eyed, still lived there (if it could be called a life) with her two children, Christopher and little Elizabeth. Not so little now, baby Elizabeth had surprised everyone by thriving – not least her mother, who had entirely neglected her, and her home, after the loss of her husband and son.

Little Robert had disappeared the day Elizabeth

had been born. He had been a bright, beautiful boy, but now he was gone. No one knew if he had been killed, or taken. Everyone had hunted for him that day, with increasing panic. Robert had spent three full days and nights searching the hill and forest. Nothing, no sign. He'd finally collapsed, exhausted, and had to be carried home.

Elizabeth and Robert hadn't talked much after that day, and he never looked at his grotesque baby daughter. Eventually, one day, he took his few possessions and left without a word. Too tired nursing the colicky infant and caught up in her grief for little Robert, Elizabeth didn't bother trying to find him. Then, Christopher had come home with the news that his pa had moved in with Anne at her house in Pendle.

Filled with rage, Elizabeth headed straight up the hill into the village to West Lane. She stopped outside the tidy cottage that Anne called a home and screamed and cursed.

'Annie! Robert! You can't do this to me, to us.' She rapped on the wooden door loudly. She peered through the small window, but it was obscured by shutters.

'You were my sister. You must come out and speak to me.'

She didn't know how she knew, but something told her that they were home and that only increased her anger. Not only had they betrayed her, but they would not even answer.

'I curse your blood! You will never be happy.' Elizabeth resumed her banging on the door, oblivious to the fact that some of the other villagers had left their houses and were watching, some aghast, some entertained.

It was only when Elizabeth began kicking the door that the miller, Jack Straw, pulled her away.

'I'm not sure if it's right, what they've done, but you can't do this, Mistress Southern. You need to go.'

Elizabeth tore her arm out of his grip – she had seen the door move and there, there was Anne.

'Annie. Why?'

Anne didn't answer. Her face showed no contrition, only pity. Anne's own husband had died of a fever years earlier, and her family – Anne and her two girls, Bessie and Anne – had struggled since then. A tiny burst of thought appeared in Elizabeth's mind – had Anne, her old childhood friend, her sister, used that dark magic on purpose? Had she lied to her, caused the death of little Robert so that she could take Elizabeth's husband? After all this time, was this revenge for Elizabeth's marriage all of those years ago?

Anne shook her head and closed the door, and Jack Straw escorted Elizabeth away.

After that, with her husband gone and no money coming in, and now no friend to turn to, Elizabeth had turned to begging as her only source of income. Her hair, which had been her best feature – black, curly and full – turned white and began falling out in clumps. The baby, Elizabeth, would have died had it not been for the care of her brother, Christopher. When things got too much and Elizabeth began spending the money she had begged on mead, a grim parody of her mother-in-law, Christopher always made sure the baby was fed. As a small seven-year-old, his huge, swimming eyes encouraged charity from passers-by much more than for his haggard mother and malformed sister, so he could always get some bread or milk.

As Elizabeth got older, she became a boisterous, determined girl. Her mother gradually gained the nickname Demdike in the village, a local word for a dirty, begging woman, and so Elizabeth reclaimed her name, having previously been 'the baby' or 'the girl' to avoid confusion. Villagers treated her with distrust and fear; it seemed Anne had spread the tale of the curse on that fateful day, and with the death of Agnes Southern, the disappearance of baby Robert and the girl's malformed face, the evidence was too much to ignore. Tie in the fact that her husband had abandoned her and, well, it was clear that Demdike was in cahoots with the Devil. Elizabeth and Demdike were avoided where possible, or spat at if they couldn't be ignored. Elizabeth, having had to deal with this behaviour for her whole life, reacted with anger and would shout and spit back. Any pity the villagers may otherwise have had dissolved at this reaction.

Fortunately for Anne, the villagers also viewed Robert's behaviour as acceptable under the circumstances. Normally, an adulterer and his mistress would be shunned and shamed, but Anne and Robert were treated like any other married couple. Anne was as trusted and loved in the village as any other wise woman; they relied on her. She could cure when the villagers couldn't afford a doctor, she could heal a cow or a goat, she could even bring wealth and happiness.

It wasn't fair. Old Demdike had had the same training. She could have been a wise woman, earned money and brought up her family better. But no.

Robert began to look well; when he'd lived at

Malkin Tower, and drank heavily every day to escape the reality of his life, he'd aged quickly. Now, his face fattened out and he began to rebuild muscle from farm work. His clothes, which had been ragged, were mended or replaced. He was enjoying his new life. He and Anne raised her children, Bessie and Anne, and ignored Elizabeth and her two children if they saw them in the village.

One day, in the December of the year that Elizabeth turned sixteen, she returned to Malkin Tower in a fury. She slammed the front door behind her, the wood rattling in protest. Demdike looked up from her spot by the hearth, the same chair her mother-in-law had died on. Unlike her mother-in-law, Demdike always insisted on a fire, whenever she could. The day she'd spent on the hill all those years ago had chilled her bones; she was sure she would never be warm again. So one of Elizabeth's jobs was to climb the hill to the forest every day to gather wood for her mother's fire.

'Not so loud, Elizabeth.' Demdike frowned. 'What is it now?'

Elizabeth was unable to reply for a while. She stomped over to the fire and sat at Demdike's feet, her head between her raised knees, breathing hard. As she had grown older, Elizabeth's facial abnormality had grown more pronounced. One eye – the left eye – was now almost an inch higher than the other. Her other eye was sunken, almost entirely hidden by the eyelid, and her mouth on that side drooped. Her chin was sunken, towards her neck – it looked crushed (occasionally, Demdike wondered whether it had been, during the labour). She walked with an odd, loping stride, her right leg dragged. She was big and blundering, but with that came strength.

'Elizabeth?' Demdike asked. She had little real affection for her daughter, saw her as the cause of all that had happened to her, the embodiment of that curse, but still – Elizabeth was her daughter, and they were in this together. Christopher, now a strong man, worked as a labourer for the Nutter family at their farm, and was courting a girl in the village. Of the family, he was the only one treated with sympathy by the villagers. He was handsome, strong, charming – of course he was treated with kindness. He would be gone soon, Demdike was sure, he would be married, and so she needed Elizabeth by her side.

'The boys,' Elizabeth said eventually, between gasping breaths.

'The boys?'

Elizabeth was being hounded by three boys in the village. They chased her, pelted her with rotten food and worse, if they could they would trip her up and they shouted insults. Elizabeth could handle this – they were no different from the rest of the village, just a little more constant and insistent – so they must have done something much worse this time.

'What did they do now?' Demdike asked calmly. Looking closely, she could see that her daughter was more dishevelled than normal, and her dress was torn. Elizabeth raised her head towards her mother, who saw that there was a large purple bruise blooming under her left eye.

'I went to the village. I was begging for a penny, just minding my own business by the side of the road,' Elizabeth said quietly. 'The boys came over, shouting and jeering. Henry Mitton. James Robinson. John Device. I shouted back and got up to leave. They followed me, close behind, until we were out of sight of the village. Then they started grabbing me, so I started running. They chased me and James tripped me up, I fell and they held me down, I couldn't move, then...' Elizabeth trailed off.

There was a long pause.

'Did they...?' Demdike asked.

Elizabeth nodded silently.

Initially, Demdike was filled with a fury which matched her daughter's. She paced the room, muttering curses, thinking quickly. There was no point in telling the magistrate; even if they were found guilty, there would only be a fine to pay. Then, she had an idea. It came to her suddenly and she froze. It was clear that Christopher would be leaving the village soon, and Elizabeth needed someone to look out for her. Elizabeth would never be able to get a husband, looking like she did, unless...

'Elizabeth, listen to me, did they all do it? Or did one hold back?'

'I don't know,' Elizabeth muttered, shaking her head, shaking all over.

'Think, girl! You were there! This is important!'

'I suppose, I suppose John didn't. I think he just watched,' Elizabeth said at length, finally looking up at her mother. Her eyes were steady, but full of tears.

John Device was from a God-fearing family. He was ordinary-looking, nothing special, and Demdike suspected he was a bit dim. No loss to his family then. He had older brothers too, if she remembered rightly, so there would be others to inherit the family business. Perfect.

'Get up, girl, we need to go and pay a visit to his family.'

Elizabeth furrowed her brow. 'What are you doing?'

Old Demdike pulled at her daughter's arm until she stood. They had to go now, or it would be too late. Elizabeth stopped protesting and followed her mother. In spite of her neglect, Elizabeth trusted her. They stormed up the path into the village, the long walk taking half the usual time due to Old Demdike's rage. A mirror of another angry walk she had taken, another time. They arrived at the Devices' house, close to the crossroads. It was a smart-looking cottage; they obviously took care of it. He was Pendle's butcher, the father, and clearly did well with his trade. Demdike rapped on the door.

'Get out here, Mother Device!' she yelled. There was movement in the village behind her as people stopped to watch. She needed an audience.

The door opened a little and Demdike saw terror flash across the face of the woman in front of her. Like her house, Mother Device looked clean and well maintained. Her hair was smooth and neatly tucked into her headscarf. Her skin, although tanned from the sun, wasn't pockmarked or peeling. Perhaps, in another life, Demdike would have looked like this. Happy, healthy and secure. But that wasn't the way her hand had been dealt.

'Your son has just attacked my daughter. Look at her!' Demdike gestured to Elizabeth's ripped dress and bruised face.

Mother Device shook her head nervously and tried to shut the door. She knew her son enjoyed taunting the girl, but surely not this? Demdike slammed her hand onto the door to stop it from closing.

'Your son has deflowered my daughter and now they need to marry.'

The crowd behind them began to chuckle. The idea was preposterous, even if he had raped the girl. Elizabeth glanced at her mother, embarrassed. What did she think she was doing?

Demdike turned to face the crowd. 'These two shall be married, or I shall call my familiar to wreak revenge on you all. Mother Device, I have a clay figure in your form at Malkin Tower. If these two do not marry, I shall stick pins in the eyes so you no longer see, I shall break off the legs so you can no longer walk and I shall claw out the tongue so you can no longer talk.'

Five days later, Elizabeth and John were married. Mother Device had been so terrified by the threat that she had agreed immediately, tears flooding down her cheeks; she had begged Demdike to treat him well. The villagers who had witnessed the altercation avoided Demdike like the plague now, lest they catch it, and even those who weren't there had been told. Witches lived at Malkin Tower.

Elizabeth didn't want to be associated with one of the awful boys who had tried their best to make her short life a misery, but she went along with it, having no other options. And, worse still, all of those things her mother had said. Things about curses and clay figures. Frightening things, which were definitely wrong. Elizabeth didn't go to church often, but she'd been enough to know that it wasn't right. Such talk was the work of the Devil.

5

An innocent child
  Skip and fall
  Is there innocence
  When the Devil dances?

1601

'Make a deal with the Devil,
  With the Devil,
  With the Devil,
  You'll pay it back one hundredfold,
  One hundredfold,
  One hundredfold,
  Make a deal with the Devil;
  You'll pay.'
The children were singing it outside Malkin Tower
again. The number and names of the children often

changed, but they had taken to playing a game near the house. They would sing the song, seeing who could get closest to the house. Old Demdike, disturbed by the irritating chant, heaved herself outside and the children immediately fled, screaming.

Fortunes for the family were going up and up. It had happened quietly first of all, back when Elizabeth had married John. It seemed that some of the villagers were so scared following Demdike's outburst at the Devices' house that they would leave gifts of food outside the house, to make sure no evil came their way. Of course, it was completely anonymous – no one would be seen offering kindness to the Southerns – but still, there was the food, left by the door.

As time wore on, the Southern family's reputation spread. John, initially horrified at what had happened to him, noticed that people had begun treating him differently, almost with respect.

The first few months of his marriage had been terrible. To start with, he had tried to pretend that it hadn't happened, even though he had been forced to move to Malkin Tower, against all custom. Normally, Elizabeth would have moved into his family's house, or they would have got a house together themselves. But neither of those happened, despite his best efforts. His own mother had been extremely forceful about his move to Malkin Tower and he had had to agree; the curse was too terrifying to contemplate. His mother avoided him, mostly, now, and he'd done the best he could to make living at Malkin Tower positive. He was, at heart, a kind man and wanted an easy life. Not that he got exactly that at Malkin Tower – but still, it was better to get on with things, do some honest labour and put food on the table for Elizabeth and Old Demdike. He'd never quite understood why Old Demdike had chosen him over the other boys who'd attacked Elizabeth that day. He knew he hadn't hurt her as much as the others, so why punish him? He never understood that what Old Demdike was looking for was kindness.

Elizabeth had been quiet, deferential to begin with, but as time wore on he saw the bright twinge of intelligence behind her eyes. Her quick nature became attractive to him; being married to her was not the chore he had once imagined.

One day, a year or two into his marriage, a man John had never seen before had sidled over to him at the tavern where he was sitting with a glass of strong ale, after a long day of labouring. The man obviously didn't want to be overheard, and had whispered some garbled nonsense in his ear.

John was tired; the farmer had wanted to relay his stone walls and it had taken a long time. His muscles ached, and he wanted peace and quiet.

'What are you muttering about?' he'd asked loudly.

The man had looked alarmed and gestured outside. Seeing as it didn't look like he intended to cause him harm, John followed the man outside and down the quiet jennel just to the side of the inn.

'You John from Malkin Tower?' the man had asked.

He looked shabby, but not poor – he was well fed.

'What of it?' John had said. He was apprehensive suddenly.

The man looked on edge, as though he knew he was doing something wrong. He would only meet John's eyes briefly, his creased, brown eyes flitting between his hands and a spot somewhere to the left of John's head.

'I need something... I can pay!'

'What do you need? I'm a labourer.' John could lay a hedge or fix a wall, scythe crops at harvest, anything to get money in. Nothing that would require a secret conversation down an alley.

'Help. I need some help. From… from Old Demdike. Or your wife.' The man now refused to meet John's eyes altogether. His hands were visibly shaking.

'Why don't you ask them?' John asked, now completely bemused.

Elizabeth and Demdike did some women's work, making cures for fevers and helping in child-birth, that sort of thing. Nothing out of the ordinary.

'I need help… getting rid of a neighbour. I heard they can… curses…'

John had laughed at the man, left him standing outside the inn and carried on with his day. But as time went on, more and more requests came in and Old Demdike did little to refute the rumours. She once took payment to sour a hated landowner's milk, and lo and behold it had worked. Although she didn't agree to many requests, John began to notice that she was building a reputation.

The fear was constant, and the villagers would do almost anything Old Demdike asked – she was careful not to ask for much, but were she to need some eggs, or a quart of ale, there was no shortage of people willing to provide it.

John and Elizabeth, surprisingly, had a comfortable and fairly loving marriage. By now they had had six children, two surviving. Alizon was a simple, gentle girl of ten and James was the opposite – twelve years old and wild. His parents could not control him and he did as he wished – thieving, fighting and damaging property. He got away with most of this, given the reputation of his family in the village.

Old Demdike ruled over this little family in Malkin Tower. Christopher had gone to live in Whalley with his wife years ago, and they rarely saw him, so it was just Old Demdike, Elizabeth, John, Alizon and James. But even without Christopher, the house felt full and busy as it hadn't for years. There was love there, in that hovel. Maybe for the first time since it had been built.

The house itself was much the same as it had always been: two rooms, one a general living space with the fireplace and some chairs, the other a bedroom where John, Elizabeth, Alizon and James slept. Old Demdike had a mat in the living room where she spent the nights by the fire.

The house was chaotic and filled to the brim.

Although the adults disapproved of James's thefts, they never returned anything he stole. As a result, they had piles of clay pots, woollen cloaks, tools and anything else James could find. Outside the house, littered around the yard, were mounds of broken farm equipment and piles of battered buckets, spits and broken fencing panels.

At the back of the house, Elizabeth had tried to revive the old herb garden but she lost interest quickly, so it was mainly weeds again. But, there were enough herbs that Old Demdike could spend her days teaching Elizabeth (with Alizon, wide-eyed and worried, peering round walls at them) the half-forgotten skills that Anne's grandmother had taught her, and the words from the abbot – secret rituals and chants, in the smoky haze of burning incense.

John tried to carry on going to the village church every Sunday, and he took James and Alizon with him. He had explained to Old Demdike and Elizabeth how important the Queen thought it was for everyone to go to church and learn and study the new Protestant religion. Old Demdike had been to church last when she was married to Robert, and hadn't felt the need to return after that. The rituals felt wrong; the new religion didn't feel safe to her. She felt secure with the old, forbidden ways, the ways she'd learned from the abbot decades before.

Having John in the house also gave Old Demdike access to information about the villagers. John had shared the news of the death of Robert, seemingly from a disease of the lungs, and Old Demdike felt a twinge of nostalgia for the life she'd once had with him. The life before that fateful day. The life before Elizabeth. With two perfect little boys. The past, a haze of golden sunshine and laughter; hate melted away with time. The memory of her mother-in-law dissolved into nothing, and Old Demdike could almost feel the gentle hug of her youngest son once again. John explained that Anne didn't go to church either, and that wasn't much of a surprise. Old Demdike knew the burning of the abbey had affected the woman she'd once called her friend as much as it had affected her. She was still a celebrated herbalist in the village, everyone loved Old Annie. Old Demdike hadn't spoken to her since the day she'd cursed her in the street after Robert had moved in. She would never forget the pain Anne had put her through.

Still, the family were happy and content now, rubbing along as best they could. John was a grounding influence on Elizabeth and Old Demdike, who flew into raging rows sometimes, and Old Demdike helped Elizabeth and John with raising their children, particularly the tearaway, James. And John continued to take the two children to church, a simple way of both building intrigue whilst also fielding suspicion about the family's skills. The absence of Old Demdike and Elizabeth was noted. The presence of John, James and Alizon was also noted. John's conscience was at ease, and the children were happy to have some contact with other people, with the outside world.

One dry April day, James persuaded Alizon to go foraging with him in the forest. They followed the road up towards the village, and just before they reached it they turned a sharp left and up the track which wove up the side of a hill. Gradually, the undergrowth became thicker and thicker until they entered the forest. Alizon took the walk slowly, stopping often to admire butterflies, birds or rabbits. She picked a blue flower (she could never remember the names) to give to her mother. James darted ahead, running forward, then back to Alizon, then forward again, like an eager puppy.

When they had collected a basket full of wild garlic, James declared, 'This is boring. I have a better idea.'

'I know all about your ideas, James. I think we should go home and give the leaves to Ma. Maybe she'll make soup with that ham Mister Dudley gave her for all that business.'

'You mean the stolen sheep?'

'Yes, Farmer Henry certainly got his comeuppance for that.' Alizon swung the basket absent-mindedly arm to arm. Some leaves fluttered to the floor, and she bent down to pick them up.

James kicked the basket from her arm in frustration. It split, cutting Alizon's arm and spilling the leaves.

'James!' Alizon cried. 'You hurt me!' She lifted her arm to inspect the cut, which fortunately was fairly shallow. There was enough blood to thrust into James's face though. 'Look!'

James smirked. 'I said, I have an idea. Are you coming, or are you running home crying?'

Despite all of his bullying, Alizon idolised her brother. He was quick and strong and clever – all of the things she felt she wasn't. He had protected her too, from the other children in the village. Alizon, being quiet and meek, had been shouted at and taunted. Perhaps she had too much of a resemblance to her mother, who had also been bothered by people in the village.

The villagers weren't afraid of her as they were of the rest of the family – although they would never push it too far and invoke the family's wrath.

When Alizon had gone to the village to try to buy some thread one day, she had walked across the crossroads and felt a thump on the back of her head. She whipped round to see a group of children keeled over laughing about twenty feet away. At her feet were the remains of a rotten apple – she ran her hand through her thick, dark hair and found that the rest of it was there.

The children started jeering and moving closer. Alizon had stepped backwards, stumbled and fallen, to the further mirth of the children. They came closer and closer while Alizon cowered in the mud, waiting for a fist or a foot.

None came – seconds later, James had thundered down the street, arms flailing. The children had backed off and begun to disperse, but James caught one, a boy of about seven, and flung him to the floor. He stamped on the boy's arm, Alizon screaming at him to stop, until the crack was audible. Alizon was never bothered by children in the village after that.

'What's your idea, James?' Alizon asked. She sucked at her arm, but she wasn't cross any more.

Instead, there was a burning feeling of excitement in her gut. James always had the best ideas. She tried her best to hide it.

James grinned. He had got his way, as usual. 'We need to go down to the village,' he said.

Alizon recoiled a little in fear. Going into the village still meant going near those people who sometimes shouted things, or gave her strange, wary glances. She wasn't sure she wanted to go. Particularly on a quest with James, the troublemaker, and without her father, whose presence stopped it.

But James was already dancing on down the hill; the discarded basket lay at Alizon's feet. She mustered her courage, picked up the basket and raced after the older brother she would always follow.

'What are we doing in the village, James?' Alizon asked when she had caught up with him.

James flashed her a bright smile. Always full of boundless energy, was James.

'I've seen something. I want it. You can help me get it.'

'What is it? Is it good?' Alizon, sweet, innocent Alizon, would never guess what James had planned.

'You know Old Annie?'

Alizon nodded. Everyone knew Old Annie.

She was the one everyone went to when they needed medicine or a blessing or some luck. That is – everyone apart from Alizon's family. They never went near the place. She knew there was an old problem, an old rippling evil that hadn't been explained to her.

'Well. I was in the village the other day. Doing this and that. And I heard a bit of a commotion round by her house.'

Alizon was already transfixed.

'So, I went round – if you go all the way down the road, you can cut back through a field and round behind her house. So I ended up in her garden, you see. I was crouching there, there's a door at the back that goes into the herb garden and I thought I'd have a look. It was open a bit. There was a right row going on in there!'

'What was going on?' Alizon asked. The idea that James had got close to these forbidden people was exciting. This was a window into another world, one where they weren't welcome.

'I'm not certain, right, but Master Nutter was there, you know with the big farm over the way, and he was screaming and shouting. He was saying something about a cow that's died, and he'd paid Old Annie to cure it.'

Alizon nodded. It happened. Old Demdike did that sort of thing sometimes, usually when whoever needed it couldn't afford Old Annie, and sometimes it didn't turn out how the person expected. Maybe Old Annie had killed the cow on purpose, maybe she just wasn't as good as Old Demdike. She guessed it was probably the latter.

'But that's not all!' James continued excitedly. 'He stopped shouting about the cow and started shouting about his pa! Says he's ill, about to die, and it's all Old Annie's fault!'

Alizon gasped audibly. Murder! Surely not. Even she knew about witches. Of course, no one minded wise women helping out, but murder? That was a different matter entirely.

'That's not everything! There's more. The reason we need to go there is, Old Annie was fussing and muttering something about a cure. She said she had something special, something no one had ever seen, but it was really powerful and amazing and all that, and she got out this sort of red box, it looked a bit soft, and showed Master Nutter whatever was in it. I tried to see, but I couldn't lean that far. Old Annie muttered some more, I couldn't hear, and Master Nutter stopped shouting. He sort of went all stiff and nodded. Tipped his cap and left. Whatever it is must be really special.'

Alizon's mouth was open now. She was thinking and thinking about what could be in the box. Gold? Some sort of other treasure? Maybe a brooch! Pearls?

'Anyway,' James continued, pleased with the look of awe on Alizon's face, 'I saw where she put it, she had to move a bit of the wall by the hearth, and I want it. She normally goes out now, and I want to see if it's there.'

'But that's stealing!' Alizon cried. 'I don't like that. It's a sin!'

James rolled his eyes. 'It's not, not when it's Old Annie. You don't know what she did to our family.'

Alizon waited, eyes wide.

'Ma and Uncle Christopher, they had a brother once. But when he was a boy, Old Annie killed him, took him away from the well and murdered him in the woods. It was awful, she did it for his insides, she needed the guts of a boy to do her spells!'

Alizon, never once doubting her brother, never once believing that he could fabricate or lie to her, was aghast.

'I never knew! Why wasn't she hanged?'

'Oh, she's clever, she is. Maybe she bewitched someone, I don't know, but no one caught her. She's got away with it for all these years. And she bewitched Old Demdike's husband. So I reckon our family deserves what's in that box. She owes it to us.'

Alizon agreed. Everything James said made sense. Old Annie did owe her treasure to them. That was clear. The idea of her murdering a little boy, a little child, especially her own uncle, was hideous. There was just one thing.

'How do you know Old Annie normally goes out now? What if she's there? She might do the same to us!'

James smiled to himself. It was so easy. Alizon didn't know anything. He ignored her question and bounded on ahead. He led them off the path, and through the forest. It was a shortcut to the field they needed to cut through to get to the old hag's house.

Alizon followed, trying her best to keep up with her smaller legs. She scrambled over branches and ducked under leaves and worried about the dangers they were heading towards. But, she couldn't help but follow.

When they got to the field, James motioned

to Alizon to follow him around the wall where they wouldn't be spotted. They picked and crept their way across the field, empty save for a chewing milk cow, whose eyes followed them without curiosity, and over the last wall into Old Annie's garden. It was neat and orderly, nothing like their garden. There were separate patches with carefully tended herbs and vegetables. It smelled fresh and bright.

James beckoned Alizon over to the back door. It was open a little, just like it had been in James's story. Alizon, although frightened, couldn't quell her rising curiosity so she crept over and peered, just a little, around the door.

The house was laid out differently to theirs. Through this door was a big central room. There was a hearth against one wall (this must be the hearth the thing was hidden near) and another fire in the middle. There was a huge pot on the middle fire, and herbs were hanging from the ceiling, drying out. There were strange symbols and vials and bones around the room. Her fear grew again.

The room looked empty. James, filled with adrenaline, took the opportunity. He rushed into the room, quietly as he could, and hastened towards the hearth. He removed the piece of stone he had seen Old

Annie move, thrust his hand into the gap and – ha! – the box was there. He pulled it out, quickly replaced the stone and headed back out of the door. He beckoned to Alizon again to follow but, just as they were crossing the garden, they heard a thud in the house. Looking back through the now fully open door, they saw that the stone had fallen from its hole. An internal door suddenly opened and they saw the outline of a woman – maybe it was Old Annie's daughter – before James grabbed Alizon's arm and they ran, ran, ran across the field, the woman's screams following them.

The children did not stop running until they arrived back at Malkin Tower, panting for breath. Old Demdike was at home, but their parents were not.

Old Demdike looked up as they flew through the door and noted first the flushed faces, and second the box in James's hands.

'Sit down and take a breath, children,' Old Demdike said, gesturing to the ground beside her chair, 'calm yourselves down.'

They did as they were told. Alizon met her grandmother's eyes and burst into tears. The fright and shock of having nearly been caught had finally caught up with her.

'Talk to me, little one,' Old Demdike said, her eyes fixed on the red velvet box.

Gasping, Alizon began, 'we went... we went... we went to—'

'We took this from Old Annie,' James cut in. He seemed afraid to open the box, now that he had it. It had some strange symbols on the top, and it felt odd. It felt strange. It had an energy to it.

Old Demdike stretched out her wrinkled hand and James, unusually, meekly handed it over to her. She ran her fingers over the strange, gold inscription. Then, ever so gently, she eased the top off the box.

'What is it?' James asked apprehensively.

Old Demdike unfolded a piece of cloth which lay on top of the contents. Then, she saw it. Time stilled. The room felt empty. Years became seconds. It was grey, ever so old, but still entirely and unmistakably a human skull. A small plaque lay underneath. On it, some writing. Old Demdike did not know many words, but when she was a child she had learned by recognition a few at the abbey. These words, she recognised them. She had seen them many times. They took her back, back to another place. The markings meant 'Abbot Paslew'.

Old Demdike thrust the skull back into the box

and closed it quickly, then dropped it down to the floor. She closed her eyes. Surely it wasn't possible? Surely Annie couldn't have taken the skull of the abbot? It was sacrilege, it was awful, he couldn't get to Heaven without his head.

'Whose is it?' James asked, staring open-mouthed at the box.

Old Demdike opened her eyes and slowly turned her head towards her grandson.

'Sometimes, lad, we do things in life that might displease God. I do. Everyone does. Once, we could be forgiven. We could tell a priest, and he would take our sins. Now we can't. It's been taken away. It's non-sense.' Old Demdike was getting angry, rambling a lit-tle bit. The words she wanted to speak were jumbled; the meaning wouldn't find its way out.

'Yes, but what does it mean?' James asked again. He had grown up in a time when there was only, officially, the Protestant religion. He had been to church often with his father, and had learned so much about that religion and the evilness of the one that pre-ceded it. The only things he knew about the old reli-gion were the secret, hidden things Old Demdike and his mother did in private. Strange hand gestures, mystical chanting, hypnotising smells of burning herbs. It felt frightening, sometimes.

'Did you know I was once friends with Annie?' Old Demdike asked, her eyes glazing over a little as she slipped into nostalgia. She had to pass on this knowledge, had to share this with the children. It was important. She felt it.

James and Alizon both nodded their heads, but Old Demdike didn't look at them and continued, talking to herself more than her grandchildren.

'We lived together once. We were the best of friends. After my mother died, she took me in. But I see now that all of that was a lie too. She has done something evil, and now I see that's the reason why everything's gone right for her all these years. People don't spit at her in the village. No one throws things, or shouts. People respect her. But I see why now. She's got the Devil on her side.' Old Demdike's tone suddenly changed; she spoke low and quickly. 'Children, this here' – she gestured at the box – 'is an evil charm. It will bring power and wealth, of that I'm sure, but only because the Devil is in charge. Does she know you have this?'

James shook his head, but Alizon nodded.

'Well? Which is it? Yes or no?'

'She did see us. Someone saw us. Not Old Annie. Someone else in the house,' Alizon stuttered.

'She knew it was you? She recognised you?

'I… I don't know,' Alizon replied. She looked bereft, exhausted.

'No,' James said. Old Demdike nodded slowly and he carried on. 'They know it's been taken but they can't know it was us. They would be here already if they did.'

'You are right, James, but they will suspect it was you. I expect we will find out how powerful this is now. Who does the Devil serve, after all?' Old Demdike glanced every now and then at the box by her feet. She looked old, older than the sun, and pale.

James and Alizon exchanged a look. Were they supposed to answer? Alizon felt tremors running up and down her spine. She was shivering, despite her close proximity to the fire, and she knew something bad had happened. She felt revulsion towards the little red box. Mention of the Devil had chilled her. More than anything, she wanted to do the right thing and not displease God. That was what they were told at church. That was what they had to do. And she always tried to do that. But it seemed that today she had done a very, very wrong thing. Maybe there was no way back from it. The fear weighed her down until she cracked and burst into tears.

James and Old Demdike ignored her. Old Demdike had her eyes shut, maybe she was in a different time again. James was peering at the box, a little smile dancing around his mouth. He looked up at Old Demdike, then surreptitiously reached a hand out towards the box. Old Demdike, without opening her eyes, leaned down and slapped it away.

'I'll be minding this, boy.'

James glowered, stood up suddenly and stormed from the building. Alizon did not even look up. Her tears dropped to the floor, pocking the earth.

Old Demdike thought on, centuries glazed on her face, her eyelids fluttering and her forehead creasing in the remembrance of things past.

6

Perhaps perhaps
Blood will flow
Perhaps perhaps

1601

Things were getting strange. Yes, of course, it had never been normal living at Malkin Tower, but it had been comfortable, even enjoyable at times. But since last year, things had gone odd. It started small, with that job when he was alone in the field and the sheep had all turned against him and that ram had gone for him... still, he'd survived and that was that.

Then the wall caving down, just where he was walking, and whether it was God's blessing or luck or who knows what that it didn't quite hit him, just his foot, so he'd been out of work for weeks.

Then the storm – no one had seen a storm like that before, and no one did seem to see it, that was the funny thing, and no one had been around – he had been on the hill, up mending some fences, and then it'd come down on him like God's judgement, hailstones the size of apples and lightning that chased him down to the forest… and now, these black dogs everywhere, staring and growling when he got close, chasing him into corners, and then as soon as he closed his eyes tight ready for the bite they disappeared, until the next one… and the screaming in the night, screaming and screaming like a newborn or a half-murdered something, or an owl (surely it wasn't just an owl?), it couldn't be just an owl because of the blood, remember, the pools of blood on the street and on his pathway and in his eyes, always in his eyes whenever he rubbed them… won't go away, won't stop, can't carry on like this.

Can't carry on.
Can't carry on.

7

Love and light and
  Hate and darkness
  Watch me leap and hold
  And harness

1603

The wind shrieked and groaned all night. Part of the roof had come away again and was banging against the rest of it, but Alizon knew that there was no point in trying to fix it until the storm passed. Malkin Tower was always half torn down by some storm or other, and ever since her pa had died, very little had been done to fix it up again. Well, James was always out, away, up to mischief probably (some things never changed), so he would never do it. He'd come back to Pendle now and then, in between bouts of who knows what.

Maybe he'd been in prison, for all she knew (and for all he told her – nothing). And then poor Old Demdike, who knew how old she was now? Mostly blind in one eye and never moving from the fireplace. Muttering to herself with that Godforsaken empty box under her chair. All her hair was gone, mostly, and anything that was left was the colour of a dirty storm-filled sky. And her own mother, Elizabeth; well, the less said about her the better. Since the death of her husband (and, all being said, it was a strange death) she had been a different woman. Angry, snapping, jumping at the smallest thing. She was so distracted she wouldn't notice if the whole roof flew off, even if she was at home. It was quite clear to her that a death like that could only have been caused by a curse, and who else would curse their family, other than Old Annie?

Of course, it was understandable. The death of her da had been a shock to them all. Alizon had only seen the briefest glimpses (Old Demdike and Elizabeth had held fort over the whole thing), but it seemed that he had died because of the skull. It had to be linked somehow. Only a few months after James had stolen it, Old Demdike had started screeching in the night that the box was empty. And so it was: the red box was there, but there was nothing in it at all. It lived under

Old Demdike's chair, and she never moved from her chair, so everyone was saying that spirits had taken it.

But then, her pa had got sick. It was slow at first, and it seemed like he was going mad, all the talking to himself about dogs and storms and that, but before long he couldn't move from his bed. The fever took and he rambled on and on about Old Annie and a familiar. Alizon had been too scared to stay in the room when the chanting had started; she had run off and when she came back to the house he was gone. Dead. He had been a good man, and she was sad. And when she thought about what she'd done with the skull, taking it from Old Annie's house all that time ago, she was riddled with guilt. She'd felt frozen for so long afterwards. Everything seemed to fall away – the happiness and light in their lives was gone.

That Old Annie would cast her revenge in this way… Alizon didn't want to think that she had murdered her pa. It filled her with too much horror.

And then, ever since the day that they'd buried her pa, Elizabeth had been strange too. Grief does strange things to people, Old Demdike said. There had been that time an illness caught the village and thirty or forty died but she didn't know any of them very well, only from going to church with her pa, and they would certainly avoid her. So Alizon had been immune to grief for a time. But now it had been two years since her pa had died and she still felt a headache whenever she thought of him. Life had been easier when he was there. Things were simpler. She felt the loss of him, etched into her. To her, that was grief. With James gone most of the time too, everything felt empty, changed.

To her mother, grief seemed to have led her to spend nearly every night on Pendle Hill. Climbing up at dusk, crawling down at dawn, every day her eyes looking a little less human. Alizon knew her mother had never cared about her appearance – she had been on the receiving end of too many jibes about her asymmetrical face for that – but these mornings when she came back from the hill she was ragged, bloody, torn. The misshapen sack she wore was snagged and filthy. She had twigs, branches even, in her matted hair and often she was ranting, and looked insane.

As the wind picked up that stormy night, Alizon wondered as usual what her mother was doing up there on the hill. James was not home – he could be anywhere – but at least Old Demdike was snoring in the other room. The sound, though she could barely hear it and often thought she was imagining it, gave her some comfort.

Another howling gust. Whatever part of the roof was flapping against the rest tore away, and suddenly Alizon could see the intrusive moon peering into the room, before a cloud rushed across and hid its view. Now that she was exposed to the elements, she could hear the creaking and grinding of the trees nearby, the occasional snap and crack. The wind was so strong it seemed to want to wipe her from the earth. It flew into the room and lifted the thin cover she pulled tightly over her. It bothered her ankles and shouted in her ears.

Dawn started to lift, and the wind eased, as though it had been led there by darkness, so the light chased it away. Alizon heard Old Demdike shifting in the room beyond – she always rose early – and she pulled her cover over her head (just a few minutes more) as she thought about the restless night she'd had and the restless day ahead fixing the roof.

She groaned. Coming up to twelve years old and already feeling like an old woman. She had been used to working hard for as long as she could remember. She was jealous of those rich boys who went to grammar school, learning to read and write – their lives seemed so much easier. What was the point in all of this? A few more minutes of despair before she drove herself from her bed and into the other room to help Old Demdike with her fire.

'An evil gale last night, girl,' Old Demdike muttered without turning around, struggling in the hearth.

'Yes,' Alizon replied, taking the flint and sticks from her grandmother and rebuilding the fire. 'Still, a better day today by the sounds of things.'

Alizon had meant the slackening of the wind, which had happened beyond doubt, and so was shocked to silence when Old Demdike began to laugh.

'What? What did I say?' She frowned at her grandmother. 'Why are you laughing at me?'

Old Demdike did not stop. Just carried on that horrible, hawking laughter. Had she gone insane? What should she do?

The front door opened.

Her mother stood blankly in the doorway, framed by light.

'Ma?' Alizon asked tremulously.

Elizabeth ignored her, and staggered into the room. Old Demdike stopped laughing as abruptly as if someone had just slit her throat. The slight fire spat out such a poor amount of light and yet it seemed that... it looked like...

'The child, then?' Old Demdike broke the silence.

'The child,' Elizabeth replied.

Alizon stared at her mother, back to her grand-mother, uncomprehending, then, the gloom in the room began to subside.

'Ma—' she began.

'Hush!' Elizabeth shouted hoarsely. 'Don't you understand what I've been through, stupid girl?'

Alizon trained her eyes on the bundle in her mother's arms. She hadn't been imagining it. It was moving, slowly, a tiny mewling, a baby?

Old Demdike rose slowly from her chair and Alizon watched with apprehension. But her mother had no husband. Her mother had not been pregnant, she thought. Her mother had spent nearly every bloody night for the last two years atop a hill, lucky she hadn't caught a cold, never mind... in a crash, Alizon realised how ignorant she had been. Her mother had had a lover, that much was obvious now. Had they met on the hill, or was that a lie too? It had been going on since the death of her father, if the night-time absences were anything to go by. And now, and now, and now…

She watched as Old Demdike held out her arms. Elizabeth passed the bundle to her and Old Demdike took it. She cradled the baby as thousands of babies have been cradled before, and smiled. Then;

'Hells! Get it away from me!' Old Demdike passed the child back to Elizabeth and threw her hands over her eyes. She sank back into her chair. 'Hells, hells, hells,' she muttered, kneading at her eyes.

Clearly the old woman was mad, what would they do? Alizon raised her eyes to her mother.

'Another child, then?' she said.

'The best of us all, simple one. This one will get rid of those evil foul hags that killed my husband, for ever. I know it. I asked it.' She sank to the floor, nuzzling her precious parcel, and Alizon looked on. The child whimpered, and Elizabeth thrust her breast into its grizzling mouth.

'What did you do?' Alizon asked, aghast.

'What needed to be done.' Elizabeth smiled down at the child, who was suckling greedily.

'Her name?' Old Demdike asked quietly from her chair.

'Jennet,' Elizabeth smiled, 'Jennet, Jennet, Jennet.'

'And the father?' Alizon asked desperately. 'The father?'

'Could be the Devil for all you care, stupid child. The Devil or God maybe. Maybe it's his holiness Jesus, or fucking Noah or maybe I'm just a slut. What do you want the answer to be, darling babe?' She directed this question down to the child in her arms, and smiled at her as she suckled. 'Maybe she's the one I was always meant to have.'

Alizon glanced at her grandmother, hoping for a glance in return that would say all of the things she wanted to hear: she loves you Alizon, she found the child in the street, this isn't what it sounds like.

Her grandmother resolutely stared at the fire, shaking a little. Not looking at Alizon, not looking at Elizabeth, certainly not looking at Jennet. No. Not looking at Jennet.

Alizon couldn't hold it back any longer and burst into tears. 'Oh, Ma! It's a sin to have a child outside of wedlock. Oh, Ma, I'm afraid for your soul!'

Elizabeth looked at her, the top eye and the bottom eye glowering like demons and then – 'You don't like what happens here, daughter, you can leave.

Nothing keeping you here. It's time you were wed anyway. You don't bring any money in, foraging and poaching is hardly a job. Get away from here and make a life somewhere else if you don't like it.'

Alizon reached for her mother. 'You can't mean it! I've nowhere else to go. Please say you don't mean it!'

Elizabeth made no reply. Her eyes were fixed on the baby: a scrawny, red, little thing. It wriggled and writhed as though it wanted to stand up and walk around. Its eyes were screwed up as it drank and drank, as though it would never be full.

'You don't need to leave, girl.'

Alizon's eyes flew to her mother's face, but she was not the one who had spoken. Old Demdike leaned forward in that old, crumbling chair.

'We won't make you leave. But you need to learn. We've been lax, you've been allowed to roam free, but you live here. You're one of us and you need to be proud of us. You can't be like Christopher, your uncle, that excuse for a son who never visits. And even your brother, James. They're ashamed of us, always have been I think, but you can't be. You won't be, will you?'

'No, no! I promise! I just, I just don't understand any of this. I don't know what's happening.' Alizon buried her face in her hands. She felt confused, slow at thought, her head full of sand. The status quo had been destroyed. Everything felt different now. She knew her mother was a strong woman who could be vicious, and that this viciousness had increased since the mysterious death of her father. But this was… this was too much to comprehend.

'That's our fault, too, Alizon. We haven't told you. Do you remember the skull, and everything I told you the day you took it?' Old Demdike was looking at Alizon curiously, almost with pity.

'I remember. I've tried to forget, but I remember. It scares me.' Alizon shivered involuntarily.

'You remember I told you about the skull, the reason why Old Annie is respected in the village?'

'Of course.'

'Well, that night, after you brought the skull home, while you and your brother were sleeping, Elizabeth and John asked me about it. We talked for hours, talked about what to do. Did you know that I caused Elizabeth and John to marry?'

Alizon shook her head.

'I tricked him and his family… pretended I had powers… people believed it anyway so I used it to give my daughter a husband. It was the right thing to do. John was good, and kind, but...' Old Demdike closed her eyes. She was floating into the past, those old memories resurfacing.

'But what?' Alizon asked. This was the longest conversation they had had in years. Alizon felt the mists clearing in her mind. She was getting answers at last.

A hacking cough from Old Demdike, then: 'But I think something happened that day. There's something hanging over us, something cold, and it only got worse when that skull came into this house. I feel it. I know it. We can cause things, we can do things, we can hurt things. Old Annie can too. That's how she killed your pa.' This was said abruptly. Not an accusation, a cold fact. 'We hadn't been careful, we didn't know what we could do. But now we do. Now I do. We'll come out of all this now, we'll come out on top.'

'I'm scared,' Alizon murmured, 'it sounds wrong. I don't think it's right... and where is the skull now?' How could they come out on top? Old Demdike was talking about... about manipulating things, people. And what had Elizabeth done?

'Gone. Stolen.' Old Demdike spat on the floor.

'Who cares? You think they care?' She gestured in the general direction of the village, over the hill. 'They care nothing for us. They care less than nothing for us. All my life, since I came to live in this shack with your grandfather, I've been treated like dirt, I've been treated like nothing for far longer than you've been on this earth.'

Alizon stared at her grandmother, her head a whirl, her conscience battling a fierce family loyalty. Her mother's face showed nothing, but then, it rarely did. The left eye, sitting higher in her face, was bright and round as a marble. The right eye, lower down and partially closed, hooded and in shadow, was as murky as a lake. Both of these eyes now stared back at her daughter. She said nothing though, and somehow the lack of speech bolstered Alizon's confidence.

'I didn't mean the villagers. I don't care what they think. They've treated me like dirt too, if it weren't for James who knows what they would have done to me by now? But, both of you, think, what about your souls?'

Old Demdike began laughing, the same mad laugh Alizon had heard just before Elizabeth had returned home: hacking, growling and hawking.

'Our souls mean nothing to us girl,' Elizabeth

said. Her eyes were focused on her baby now. 'We worked it out. Your grandmother and I. Our souls are dead. They were sold long ago, long, long ago, and now we have accepted our fate. We face Hell, so we may as well make sure these lives are worth living.'

Elizabeth had always had a deep, mumbling voice and Alizon had to strain to hear her words.

'Ma?' Alizon asked, her voice becoming high-pitched with desperation. 'You can't be serious? Do you know what Hell means, how it lasts for eternity?'

Elizabeth seemed to have said enough, and she looked back down at the little bundle in her arms, which appeared to be sleeping peacefully. Old Demdike spoke next.

'Old Annie sold our souls the day your mother was born. There was a trick – something I don't have the power for, something evil – and I've spent years trying to find out what she did that day. I had a sight when I touched that blasted skull, and now I know what the price was. We'll go straight to Hell when we pass, girl, and I wouldn't be surprised if you do, too. Your blood is the same. You're one of us, whether you like it or not.'

Alizon took her time to reply. She wasn't a devout girl, but she was rightly God-fearing, as everyone should be. You were on this earth for a few short years and then, before you knew it, you were dead for the rest of eternity. Alizon was certain she knew enough of Heaven and Hell to know where she would prefer to end up. The villagers muttered about witchcraft often enough, everyone was scared of the unknown and what those with evil powers could do. Alizon herself had been terrified enough of Old Annie after they stole the red box; there were whispers about what she could do. But Alizon had never thought that her family were like that.

'I don't want to go to Hell,' was all she could say.

'Well, I don't think your wants have anything to do with it, girl,' came Old Demdike's cracked reply.

The baby began to cry.

8

It bursts like blood
  Bursts forth
  It flows like blood
  Flows through

1608

Alizon was running down the street, towards the tavern. It wasn't a place that she would normally visit, but she had heard whispers that James was back, and she was desperate to see her wayward, charming brother. It had been almost six years since he'd lived full-time at the Tower, and memories of him filled her mind. His constant movement, his wide grin. She couldn't wait to see him.

Alizon kept to the shadows, always preferring to avoid attention. She passed some people in the street, but it was fairly quiet. The villagers were suspicious of her, and she was suspicious of them. She knew of them by name, remembered them from her churchgoing days, but rarely talked to them. She had experienced too much pain at their hands as a weak child and still preferred to keep her distance.

It was a wet March day, puddles deep and muddy on the road and a relentless drizzle filling the air. She was filled with excitement when she reached the door of the tavern, and hurried inside into the warm and dry.

It took a few seconds for her eyes to adjust to the dimness. There was a cheery fire in the fireplace and the ale wife was chattering loudly to a group of men sitting around a table eating stew. She looked around slowly before she spotted who she was looking for. Her brother, James – for it was undoubtedly James – was sitting in a quiet corner with another man. Alizon rushed over, her heart happy and light.

'James!' she exclaimed, throwing her arms around his neck.

James put down his tankard and smiled broadly. 'Alizon,' he said. He returned her embrace, stood and offered her his chair, then waved at the ale wife who brought over another tankard of ale.

'You look wet,' James said.

Alizon scoffed. 'You've had me wading through puddles! You couldn't come to Malkin Tower and save my dress?'

James shook his head as he pulled over another stool. 'Not this time.'

'Where have you been?'

'All over, wherever I can get some work. Building or working on farms mostly.'

Her brother had aged since she last saw him. His hair was unruly and already tinged with grey, as was his beard – unusual at eighteen years old. His skin was the wrinkled and nut-brown skin of a labourer, and his eyes were bloodshot. But, his clothes looked new and clean. His boots were strong and sturdy. He seemed to be doing alright, and Alizon was glad.

She turned to observe the man sitting with her brother, and felt a strange, unfamiliar connection in her chest. He had been looking at her, directly, with deep, dark brown eyes. They were so bottomless that she felt uncomfortable.

'John Robinson,' he said, and held out his hand for her to shake.

She took it, felt a firm grip and calloused fingers.

'Alizon Device,' she replied. 'Do you work with James?'

'Here and there, now and then,' he replied.

A smile was dancing around his face, and Alizon felt herself blush deeply.

'John and I have done some bits and pieces together. Something like the bits and pieces we used to do, you and I.' James raised his tankard.

Alizon slammed her tankard down on the table. 'If you mean thieving,' she looked around and lowered her voice as she said this, 'you'd better stop because it'll get you killed. And I'll have you know that I never wanted to do that, and I never have again.'

Alizon was annoyed to see that both men were laughing at her. She decided that she didn't like John, with his strange, disarming eyes, and he must be a bad influence on her brother. He seemed to be looking right through her.

'Ah, drink your beer, sister. We're not in any trouble,' James said reassuringly, raising his tankard again.

'Not in this village anyway!' John laughed.

He drank the last of his beer, and waved the ale wife over. She brought three more tankards, with a toothy smile for John. Alizon, who was not used to strong beer, had only had a few sips from her first tankard, but at James's encouragement she drank more. She was pleased to notice that the more beer she drank, the less uncomfortable John made her feel.

'Are you going to see Ma this time?' Alizon asked.

'No,' James said heavily. 'I can't work out that little one, and I'd rather stay out of it.'

Alizon nodded. How could she communicate how she felt: that she couldn't get her head around the little one either, that she wished she could just escape like James, who had only seen Jennet once on his last visit. But it was too late now. It was too late to say any of that, she knew she was already damned. Alizon glanced up and saw John staring again. She cleared her throat.

'I would say Ma would be sorry not to see you, but she's got her hands full. She's old to be running around after a five-year-old.' She tried to sound light-hearted, but the words stuck in her throat and she could feel John's curious look. She thought about trying to explain, but where to begin? There were no words to describe what was happening at Malkin Tower, the rejection she felt from Elizabeth, the discomfort, the lack of faith in God.

'Tell me about you, Alizon. Are you happy?' James asked. 'Have you got a fancy man?'

'Oh no!' Alizon laughed. 'No one in the village would want me!' Again she tried to sound light-hearted, again the words stuck in her throat. She took a long drink of beer to cover her discomfort.

'I'd imagine that lots in the village would want you,' John said slowly, leaning forward.

For a moment, Alizon felt seen. She felt her mahogany brown hair and her full pink lips. She felt her thin waist and her strong legs. Then she remembered herself. She was a dirty wench from Malkin Tower, sitting in a wet, stinking dress which happened to be her only one. John was teasing her.

'You need to get away from here, sister. What are you going to do with your life?' The look on James's face was definitely pity.

Alizon drank more beer.

'I do lots with my life, thank you! Do you think Old Demdike would still be alive if I weren't there, looking after her?'

'Old Demdike's still alive! I am glad. How old is she now? You must be doing something right. Either that or the Devil's keeping her hanging on!'

James burst into laughter and John followed suit, but Alizon just smiled tightly.

'Where are you staying?' Alizon asked, desperate to change the subject.

'John has a cottage down the road. He's renting it while we do some work. I'm paying him to stay for a while.'

A cottage down the road. Alizon felt wistful for everything that invoked. Freedom and safety and hope. All at once she felt the weight of her life at the Tower, how claustrophobic it had been since Jennet had been born. The screaming, the exhaustion, the misery. Jennet had been an unhappy baby, she was an unhappy child, and her crying had felt almost constant. Like it would never stop.

'Why don't we head there now? I have some mead and some of yesterday's stew. We can feast!' John looked at James, who nodded agreement, and at Alizon, who felt mounting excitement.

John stood up and paid the ale wife, and as he did so Alizon noticed how very tall he was. He had broad shoulders, and his hair was the same colour as hers.

Alizon stood too, aware of the mud at the bottom of her dress from wading through the puddles earlier. James took her arm to lead her down the street towards the house that John had rented. It turned out to be one of the very small cottages that was situated on the way out of the village. They were owned by the Nutters, the family of farmers, and were usually used by labourers. They always looked a little bit run down and uncared for because the occupants never stayed long, but as they approached John's, Alizon could tell that he had worked hard to make it presentable. She could see fresh timber where the window and door frames had been fixed up, and the front had been scrubbed.

John stepped ahead to open the door and usher them inside. It was gloomy. John bent down in front of the fireplace and fussed with some sticks and, before long, a crackling fire was ablaze. Alizon was surprised to see him light some candles too – they were expensive, and in a home as small as this she would never have bothered with them. But as the room (for it was a single room, though a large one) began to light up, Alizon saw that of course he had candles. Most of the room was given over to a workshop – she could see tools and piles of wood.

'What do you make?' Alizon asked, wandering

over to a large, sturdy table which was topped with all
sorts of unusual metal tools and knives.

'I'm a wood worker,' John replied.

He gave her another of those deep looks and
Alizon took an involuntary step back.

'It's alright, you can look.' John leaned over the
table and picked something up. 'Here, keep this.'

Alizon took it and looked carefully. It was a little wooden toy in the shape of a dog, delicately made
and beautiful. 'I can't keep this!' Alizon exclaimed.
She'd never really had anything of her own before, and
it felt like a gift of jewels or silk. It was too much.

'Suit yourself,' John said, and took the dog
back. He placed it onto the table and clapped his hands
loudly. 'Drink!'

He strode over to a set of shelves near his fireplace and took down a bottle and three little glasses.
This was luxury too – they didn't have glasses at
Malkin Tower. He gestured to a chair in front of the
fireplace and Alizon sat. James was already perched on
a stool right by the fire, bothering the flames with a
stick. John pulled over a stool, too, and handed them a
glass each, then filled them to the brim with the golden
liquid.

'Your health,' John raised his glass and drained

it, as did James. Alizon did the same thing, and coughed and spluttered as the burning liquid hit her throat.

James laughed. 'You need more practice!'

John filled their glasses again and Alizon was glad to see he sipped his this time. She took a small gulp and winced. She had tried mead before – she once found a bottle of Old Demdike's hidden away, but she realised now that it must have been watered down to last longer, because it had tasted nothing like this. When she got used to the taste, Alizon noticed that it was sweet, warming and nothing like the pale weak beer that they drank at home. It felt like honey trickling down her throat.

Her eyes kept straying over to the work table and the wooden dog. She was annoyed at herself for being so ungrateful, she had had a beautiful toy in her hands for such a short time, and through her own actions it had been taken away.

John and James began talking about a job they had on, and Alizon stopped following the conversation. She felt pleasantly warm and content in this little hut. The chair, although wooden, felt immensely comfortable, and she tucked her legs under herself. The mead continued to taste nicer, the more she drank. She blinked, and her glass was empty.

'That's more like it, sister!' James said.

He had the bottle now and filled her glass. Alizon felt a little sluggish, but pleasantly so. She turned to look at John. He was looking at her again.

'Can I have the dog, actually?' Alizon asked. The words were out of her mouth before she could stop them. She felt an unnatural confidence, as though she was watching herself from behind a mirror.

'His name is Night,' John said. He went to the table, picked up the wooden dog and turned it over in his hands. 'I made him after a dog I had. A good companion. He's dead now, of course.'

He passed the dog to Alizon, who took it reverently. 'Night,' she whispered. She clutched the dog to her heart. 'Thank you.'

Their eyes met again. Another of those looks. Alizon dragged her gaze back to James.

'How long are you going to be here for?' she asked, feeling energised again.

'Who can say?' James replied. 'As long as the work is here. We had a good thing going in York, but that dried up.'

Alizon didn't really want to think about what

work James meant. He could be talking about labouring, sowing crops or tending to animals, he could be talking about other, much worse things – theft, perhaps even murder. There was a part of her that wanted to ask, but she put it from her mind, and was surprised to find this easier than usual.

'I missed you when you were away, James. I wish you'd stay. Malkin Tower isn't the same without you.' Alizon's head was full of happy memories from her childhood, when their father was still alive. Alizon and James, always together, always looking out for each other, them against the world. The balance of power had all changed now.

'It's been years, sister. You can make your own life. You don't need me. You can do as you like.' James smiled over his drink at her.

'I can't. You don't understand.' Alizon bowed her head. How could she explain that she felt somehow tied to them, tied to that place, with nowhere to go? She was terrified that she was damned and stuck. Not only that, but what would she do? Women worked with their husbands, and she had no husband.

'Stew?' John interjected. He had been busying himself at the fire, and now he ladled a helping into a bowl, passing it to Alizon.

'Thank you.' She suddenly realised how hungry she was. The stew had plenty of meat in it, which was a treat – usually a rabbit was stretched out for as long as possible at Malkin Tower. When she had finished, she stood and sighed, feeling a deep sadness.

'I had better go. They will wonder where I am,' Alizon said. 'I'll see you again soon?' she asked James.

'If God wills it,' James replied, the old and familiar parting statement.

Alizon left with her dog clutched tightly in her hand. She closed the door behind her and, as she did, she heard raucous male laughter coming from inside. The thought of returning to Malkin Tower filled her with dread. She thought briefly about just leaving home: setting off in the opposite direction and walking until she reached somewhere, anywhere, that would give her work – maybe as a maid or a labourer, she would do anything. But she dismissed the thought almost immediately. She knew she didn't have the courage. The road was dangerous, with robbers and who knew what else.

Instead, she walked home in the darkness, every step heavy, until the silhouette of the Tower appeared around the hill. A ragged shadow against the pitch-black mound. As soon as she saw it, she heard Jennet's familiar screams.

9

We will crash
  And we will smash
  And by the end
  It will be done

1608

Alizon awoke to the sound of Jennet screaming, as always, in the room that she shared with Elizabeth and Jennet. Her head was sore, her mouth dry. She saw her mother standing over her.

'Disgusting,' Elizabeth muttered.

Alizon lifted herself from the pile of straw she slept on, and stumbled outside to a bucket which was full of rainwater. She splashed it onto her face and shook her head, felt a little better, then without warning vomited beside the bucket.

Elizabeth had followed her and Jennet trailed behind her, her face red and scrunched up, the wails continuing.

'Where did you go yesterday, you whore?'

Alizon squinted up at her. She desperately filtered through her memory. She remembered leaving John's cottage, she remembered some of the walk home – it had been dark, it had been night... night. Night. Without answering her mother, Alizon ran back into the bedroom and clutched through the straw. She felt wood beneath her fingers, it was there. She kept it hidden under the straw and turned around to face her mother, who had followed her inside and was looking at her with an expression of utter contempt.

'Can't you shut her up?' Alizon moaned, and immediately regretted the words.

She was answered with a slap across the face that set her head ringing. She flung herself down onto the straw, arms covering her head.

'How dare you. Tell me where you were,' Elizabeth growled, over Jennet's crying.

'Out. I don't need to tell you,' Alizon replied, more bravely than she felt. She still couldn't recall getting home. She didn't know if Elizabeth had been awake or asleep when she got back, didn't know if she'd said anything, didn't want to contradict herself. She was feeling a welling up of injustice, as if prior to last night she had been numb. All she had done for Elizabeth and Old Demdike and Jennet, to be treated as though she was a servant, or a slave.

Jennet had stopped crying.

'You have jobs to do. You need to go to the village and get supplies. Old Demdike has the money. Then you need to catch a rabbit, we need food. And the Devil save you if you come back empty handed, girl.' Elizabeth slapped her daughter once more and stalked from the room.

For once, Jennet did not follow her. Instead, she continued staring at Alizon, immobile. Eyes deep as wells. There was no expression on her face. Slowly, she moved her arm and began to suck her thumb.

For once, Alizon was glad of the excuse to visit the village. She went through to the main room, where Old Demdike was, as always, sitting by the fire.

'Don't be stupid, girl. Remember what you know,' Old Demdike said, quickly and quietly, before raising her voice to say, 'A spool of thread. A yard of cloth. Vinegar.'

Alizon shook her head at the warning, if that's

what it was, took the coins from Old Demdike (never ask where she got them from) and left the house. It was much drier than the previous day, the sun peering out from behind heavy clouds.

Leaving the house felt like leaving a weight behind her. The headache lifted, and she almost danced up the path, which was still a little muddy from the rain.

She felt strange. It was like she'd been asleep for years. It felt like she'd spent so much time covered with a blanket, and now it had been removed from her head. She could see the world. She felt disgusted by the place she lived: a feeling she had never really had before. She saw the women she lived with as sickening, small, and put this down to the meeting with James the day before. He had opened her eyes to another future. Her mother must love her – she knew that. She had never been as easy or willing to show her love as their father had been, but Alizon remembered tender moments from her childhood – a hug by the fire, a song to distract her from a grazed knee. In Alizon's mind, there were two catalysts for the change – her father's death, and the arrival of Jennet.

Her heart rose as she reached the village. She even smiled as she saw Anne Redferne, Old Annie's daughter, walking in the street; the smile was met with a grimace but Alizon didn't notice. She wondered if she would bump into James.

There was a pedlar on a corner by the tavern. He had the thread and the cloth, and pointed her to a second pedlar who had vinegar. He was on the way out of the village, very close to John's house. Alizon bought the vinegar and toyed with whether or not to see if her brother was in. She still felt courageous, so she walked up to John's door and knocked quietly.

'Come in!' a deep voice called.

Alizon opened the door and stepped into the room. A fire was blazing; the heat hit her immediately, and she could see John was working at his table.

James didn't seem to be there, so she said, 'I am sorry, I was looking for James,' and turned to leave.

At the door she felt a hand on her arm and turned back to face John.

'It's alright. Wait for him. He'll be back soon. Here, sit by the fire. Beer?'

Alizon felt herself being led to the chair. She looked closely at John. She wasn't sure if she trusted him, didn't know what he was thinking. He was obviously older than her, knew more of the world than her, as surely most people did, and yesterday it had seemed as though he was laughing at her.

But his words seemed kind today, so she sat and took the beer from him. He turned back to his work table, put his tools away, then sat down next to her with a beer of his own.

'Your health,' John said, and raised his drink.

Alizon raised hers too, and they both drank deeply. She was thirsty after her walk.

She noticed John watching her again, always watching, and wondered what he saw. They had no mirror at Malkin Tower; Alizon had rarely seen a clear reflection of herself. She knew her hair was something to be proud of – it was deep brown, darker than anyone else's in the village, and it curled naturally. Old Demdike had told her all of these things. She kept good care of it with a hairbrush James had given her, probably stolen but she hadn't asked. She knew her face was even – at least, compared to her mother's. She knew her skin had been pale, but was beginning the inevitable transition to golden from the sun. Other than that, she knew very little. He probably thought she was filthy. She normally washed in the stream, but the winter had been colder than normal. Her clothes were the ones she'd waded through mud in yesterday then slept in, not that she had any others to change into.

He, on the other hand, looked clean. His hands were dirty, from the woodwork, she imagined, but his face was washed. He was wearing different clothes today, a green shirt rather than the brown one he had been wearing the day before. His skin was tanned, his brown hair fell into his eyes. He brushed it away.

'Where is James?' Alizon asked, feeling that the silence had gone on for too long.

'I didn't ask. He comes and goes as he pleases. Sometimes he needs me, sometimes he doesn't.' He shrugged his big shoulders.

For a moment, Alizon imagined the muscles flexing under the shirt like a bull, then shook the thought from her head.

John leaned forward and she blushed.

'Such pretty colouring,' he said, and brushed her cheek with his finger.

Alizon froze. She had been touched so few times in the last few years, and rarely gently. How could his hand feel so hot?

She lowered her eyes to the floor. John lifted her chin with one finger, but she avoided his gaze.

'Tell me, Alizon, I want to know about you.'

John was almost whispering, his look so intense her mind went blank.

'There is nothing to know,' Alizon murmured.

'Of course there is,' John replied. 'You have a brother. I hear your father is dead.'

Alizon nodded slowly, repressing the memories of that time. 'A... a fever, they think.'

'I'm sorry,' John said. 'It is hard to lose a parent. My father died of a fever too, when I was just a boy. Luckily I had my uncle, he taught me my skill. What of your mother?'

'She lives at Malkin Tower, with my grandmother and sister.'

'That's a blessing then,' John replied.

Alizon looked up at him, assuming he was joking, and realised his eyes were far away. Probably he had been orphaned as a child, she guessed, like so many.

'And your grandmother and sister?' John asked, his eyebrows raised.

'What... what about them?' Alizon asked.

From John's expression, this was the wrong answer. Was it possible that he knew so little of her family? She had grown up so used to notoriety.

'I... are they well?'

It was the first time she had seen him less than confident, less than sure of himself.

'As well as can be. My grandmother is very old. Her life has not been easy. My sister is just five. It seems life has not been easy for her either.' A wry smile escaped her lips. Somehow, here, she felt separate from them.

'What do you mean?' John asked.

He was still leaning forward, listening to her with an intensity she had never experienced. Had anyone, apart from James, ever listened to her before? John picked up his jug of ale and filled her empty cup.

'She is a difficult child, I think. My mother is old, now. My father is…'

'Dead,' John finished, and filled up his own cup. 'So he died recently?'

'No… it was…' Alizon paused. She was telling this stranger more of her family than anyone else knew. But she didn't seem to care. Everything had changed. 'He died two years before my sister was born.'

'It must be hard for you,' John said.

Alizon was shocked by the response. She had been expecting a reproach, some sort of disgust. She had never really thought about her situation in terms of herself before but now, now she agreed with him. It was hard for her. No one had seen, or cared before.

'I understand they're your family. But they're James's family too. And James doesn't hang around looking after them, does he?'

John had taken one of Alizon's hands. It was sitting, unmoving, in his. The heat of him was enveloping her. She didn't want to move her hand. If she did, everything would break.

'No, but I have to. It's in my blood.' Alizon felt a pulse around her hand. She forced herself to look into his eyes. They were as dark as ever. She could see the fire flickering in them.

'What if you stayed here with me?' he asked. 'What if you were with me?'

'I can't…' Alizon started. 'I couldn't…'

But his eyes were so close. She started to think, maybe, what if… the eyes were closer now, and she couldn't think at all.

'Come with me, Alizon. Leave this place.'

His lips met hers. Her stomach flipped over. She didn't want it to end.

After what felt like an eternity, she moved away.

'I couldn't. My family.' She looked at him carefully. What would he want with her? Was this a trick?

'It is your choice, of course, but it doesn't sound as though your family care for you. I think I could make you happy. We could leave here, go anywhere you want to.'

Alizon frowned. Her head felt full, her hands were trembling a little. It made no sense, any of this. Now she felt tricked and confused and annoyed.

'You don't know me. I'm no one. From nowhere. Why would you want me with you? You could just ditch me as soon as I've left and then where would I be? In a worse scrape than I'm in now.' Alizon felt the tears well and fall before she could stop them.

'You're right. So marry me.' John smiled.

Alizon couldn't comprehend, it was all too much. It was so fast, all of this, and she was used to the luxury of thinking slowly. 'But I've known you for a day.'

'I'm sorry. You're not like anyone I've ever met. I want to learn more about you. I want to keep you safe. I want you to be happy.' John looked innocent now, his face open.

Alizon had no experience to compare this to. She had never had any attention from a man before.

She couldn't be sure of her thoughts, they were sluggish.

'You've known me for a day. Why would you want to do this?' Alizon asked. She was being given a way out of the murk and grime she lived in, but her life had been disappointment after disappointment so far and it felt too good to be true. And terrifying too.

It felt like a door was opening. A door to the life she had never truly let herself dream of: a life like those simple women in the village had, with their children and their friends, their gossip by the well and their full plates. It would still be hard work, of course, but there would be love there. Proper love, not the reluctant bond of blood her family shared.

'I told you, you're not like anyone I ever met. You're special. I've met hundreds of girls. I've never met any I want to marry. Until I met you.'

Alizon felt dizzy. John kissed her again and she knew what she wanted her answer to be. But then, another feeling – was it guilt? The reluctant bond of blood had strength. Perhaps her family would have been like those in her dreams, if it hadn't been for the poverty, the hatred and fear, the shunning from Old Annie.

'I can't tell them. I can't tell my mother and Old Demdike.' Alizon looked at her hands.

'If you don't want to tell them, Alizon, then I'll tell them. I'll do anything for you.'

That was it. That was enough. She nodded slowly and John kissed her, then a hand moved to her leg. The top of her thigh. It rested there, innocently, no pressure, but her blood knew and it rushed. It flew. Then she was on his bed, nothing could stop this, nothing would and it felt right.

Once it was done, Alizon lay back on the bed. She looked at John. He was smiling, his eyes closed. She felt very alone, separate. Ashamed, now. Another sin. She had been carried away in the moment, and clarity was returning to her.

'I suppose you want me to go and talk to your family now?' John asked.

Alizon nodded, her eyes wide, gathering her clothes back around her.

John sighed, threw his shirt and trousers back on, covering the shoulders she'd imagined, and stood.

'By the time I come back, we'll have each other and that will be that.'

And then he was gone.

10

Clockwork
  Tick tock
  The time will come
  The luck will lock

1608

Alizon sat on the chair next to the fire. The sky was getting darker outside John's cottage. Each minute that passed, she imagined where he was now. He would be approaching the Tower, if not there already... he would be talking with Old Demdike... he would be on his way back now, any moment, he would be back.

Elizabeth... well, she was a strong woman. A strong, determined woman. Her mother did what she wanted, and cared little for the consequences, or the effect on anyone else. As soon as her husband had died, she had stopped caring for Alizon and James. It was as though she had realised that however much you care for someone, you can't stop the inevitable. But then along came Jennet. The wonder child. Her special one.

Alizon had spent a long time trying to determine the father of Jennet. She had watched her mother, at a distance, whenever she had come into contact with a villager. Was that her husband? But there were never any clues. Just more silence.

Alizon wondered how they were taking the news. It must be bad, John had taken so long. She was young, and he was older, perhaps in his late twenties, but maybe they would let her go anyway. Be rid of her. She stared and stared into the fire.

The door moved.

'John?' Alizon leaped from the chair.

'What?' James replied.

Alizon returned to her place by the fire and the reality of her day sank into her mind. Had she always been a fool?

'Alizon? What are you doing here?' James hurried to his sister's side.

In a rush, the story fell from her mouth. The words tumbled over each other and James had to pick them up and put them in place.

'We have to go,' James said, swiftly, decisively. He pulled Alizon up, and out of the house, before she had a chance to stop him. His grip on her arm was firm. She had no choice.

'James!' she shouted, panic rising in her throat. 'What is it about him?'

'It's not what it is about him, fool, it's what it is about them. I'm afraid for him.'

James let go of her arm and ran down the street. Alizon chased him, but she was slower, as she always had been.

James was calling her to hurry, to run, his breath rasping as they approached the woods.

She ran as though her life depended on it, and when she reached the woods she welcomed the slowing that was necessary as she picked her way through the undergrowth.

Alizon had lost sight of James. She didn't want to call him; the woods were watching.

She paused, her body took a second to adjust to the lack of motion, and she squinted her eyes.

There, between the trees, was a shadow. She walked now, picking through the plants until she reached what she had seen. And when she got there, she dropped to her knees.

James was kneeling too. He was kneeling over… he was kneeling over John. John was lying askew on the ground, eyes open and staring upwards.

'John?' she said, shaking his shoulder. When there was no response, she said again, more frantically this time, still shaking him, 'John? John. John!'

She stopped only when James grabbed her arm. 'Stop, Alizon, he's gone.'

Alizon raised her eyes slowly. She felt completely still and empty, like a statue. 'You did this.' Her voice was ice.

James frowned at her. He began checking John, he looked closely at his head, his chest.

'He has no money on him. Nothing to steal. You did this for nothing.' Alizon began to shake, cold to her bones.

James stopped and looked at her again. 'Are you serious? You think I did this? Why would I? I could have robbed his house, if I had wanted to. This was something else…'

'You didn't like what you saw when you got to the house. You didn't like the fact that he was going to marry your sister. Admit it.' If she had a knife, she would have stabbed James. She wanted to hurt him, to see him suffer. She wanted him to curl up into the

ground, writhing in pain, and drop straight down to
Hell.

James stared at her incredulously. 'Why would
I murder him for that?'

'How should I know? Who knows how you
think? You're a murderer. I'll see you hang for this.'
Alizon imagined her brother swinging on the end of
a noose, his sly and clever eyes bulging and bloodshot,
his face growing purple.

'You have gone mad. Mad.'

There was horror on James's face, but Alizon
began to feel scared. She had to get to the village,
to tell someone, but James would never let her go.
What if he murdered her too? He could easily, she was
so much smaller than him. She glanced around for a
weapon. There were no obvious wounds on John –
it couldn't have been a rock to the head or a knife
through the heart. How else could he have done it?
Her own brother. Her only ally.

Alizon slowly began to rise. Maybe she could
get a head start back to the village. But almost immediately, James grabbed her arm hard, his fingers push-
ing deep into her flesh. She fell, landing on him, lying
across his chest, and started to cry.

'If you are going to kill me, do it now,' she

sobbed. 'Do it now so I can be with the one person who ever loved me.'

'If you think he loved you, you're even more of a fool than everyone thinks you are,' James said dully.

'He did! We were to marry!' Alizon cried through her tears.

'No. You were to marry because I told him to. He owed me – he seriously owed me. There was an… an incident, and I helped him. Saved his life really. Just before we came here. And when I saw you, how unhappy you are stuck at Malkin Tower, I thought this could be the solution. I told him to marry you. He didn't love you – not yet anyway. He was going to do it to pay me back.' James said all of this with no expression, a blank look in his eyes.

'You're lying,' she whispered.

'No. I'm not lying. He would have been kind to you, maybe would have grown to care for you, I know that. I would never have asked him to if I didn't think he would be kind. I thought you could move away somewhere, and have children. Then even if he stopped caring about my deal, the children would still bring you comfort and purpose. But now… nothing.'

Winded, Alizon stared down at John's face and then back up at James. John had been so convincing in his love. The golden day. She shook her head, trying to shake James's horrible words out of it. She shook until James grabbed her head with his hands and held it still.

'So you see, dear idiot, there would be no point in murdering him. I told him to marry you. Why would I kill him because he was going to marry you?' James said, staring into her eyes, as though he was trying to force the meaning into her head.

'This is all a lie. You're just trying to stop me from telling someone. You always had a trickster's tongue, and now you are trying to trick me.'

This was how James had always been: doing wrong things then somehow wriggling out of punishment. But she wasn't going to let him this time. He had seemed harmless before, but now she wasn't so sure.

'You believe me, Alizon. You have to believe me. Because something worse is happening. I didn't kill John, and that means that someone else did.'

James was looking panicked now. Good. He was finally realising that she was no fool, to be trodden all over.

'If you come with me to the village it will be better for you, James. You will be hanged for your crime, but if you admit what you did you might be able to make your peace with God. If you run, then you will be condemned to Hell for ever.'

Alizon tried to rise again, but James had not loosened his grip on her head. She stayed where she was. She was still crying, a little, tears dripping down her face and onto John's chest, but she felt herself fill with a righteousness. She had to get James to the village to suffer his fate. He was her brother, but in this moment she hated him.

James let go of her head to bury his face in his hands. 'We're in Hell already, Alizon, can't you see? You think this life is a joy? No money, little food.'

Alizon stood. 'I'm going to the village,' she said, as steadily as she could. 'I'm going to tell them and it would be best if you come with me. You don't want to spend the rest of your life, however long it lasts, as an outlaw.'

'Wait. I can prove it wasn't me!'

James was still on his knees. Alizon felt fury course through her.

'I won't let you trick me any more,' she replied, and began to walk away. She felt, suddenly, the weight of what had just happened crash down on her. Her one chance of happiness was gone. Strangers in Pendle were so rare, and the other men in the village treated her with fear, if they didn't ignore her completely. John was her last chance. Her brother had destroyed everything. She had cared about him, deeply, but now... now she had nothing. She had been let down, one time too many.

'Wait. How are you going to report the murder if you don't even know how he died?'

'Show me,' she said. She didn't trust herself to say any more.

'As I said,' James began through gritted teeth, 'I didn't kill him. I don't know how he died. We need to check the body together if we are going to find out.'

A trick. Always a trick.

Alizon knelt back down next to John. Looked into those deep, deep eyes which had turned shallow with death. There was no sign of injury to his face or the top of his head. He looked perfect still, apart from those empty eyes.

Her gaze slid down to those broad shoulders and across his chest, down to his stomach. There was no sign of blood. His clothes looked just the same as when she had last seen him living and breathing.

His legs were splayed at an unusual angle, but they didn't look broken. It looked more like he had fallen suddenly. Questions grew in Alizon's mind.

'How did you do it?' she muttered.

James just stared at her, lips tight.

'Help me turn him over,' she said.

Gently, Alizon placed her hands on John's side and James pulled him towards him. He turned over with a thump. John's hair was clumped with mud from where he had been lying on the ground. Alizon ran her hands through it, looking for a wound, but there was none. No cracked skull, no bleeding fissure, nothing.

'This would be quicker if you just told me what you did to him,' Alizon said, avoiding James's eyes. She noticed her brother's grim smile and it infuriated her. Her resolve strengthened with the anger, and she studied John's back, expecting to see the slash and mess of a stab wound.

There was nothing.

'Poison, perhaps? Do you know of anyone who deals in spells and mysteries and poisons?'

James smirked.

'You bought poison? From Old Annie?'

'No, I didn't buy poison. And I wasn't thinking of Old Annie either,' James said, that same expression on his face.

'Then you stole it. Who from?' For once she was able to see through her charming, conniving brother. She felt as though she had aged thirty years in the last twenty-four hours, and gained all of the wisdom that came with it.

James stared back at his sister. 'Are you purposefully not listening to me? Are you that stupid? I am telling you that your mother, your grandmother, your sister did this.'

James was trembling now, for what reason Alizon did not know. She felt his words wash off her. She had a shield that had been built of her need for James to receive punishment, and none of his lies could change that.

'So you poisoned him. You snuck poison into his beer, or his food, it would be easily done,' Alizon mused.

'You still don't understand,' James started. His voice had become strangely high-pitched. 'My God, you still don't understand. Have you ever seen someone who has died of poisoning?'

'I understand more than you think! And no, I haven't, because I don't poison everyone who crosses me. I am not a murderer, unlike you.'

James shook his head, as though he had suddenly remembered something. 'Yes you have!'

'No, I haven't.'

'You have, Alizon.' He grabbed her arm. 'Remember. When we were children. We were going somewhere – I don't remember where – and we went through Nutter farm, and we found that cow.'

Alizon shook her head. His words were nonsense. The shadows were lengthening rapidly, creating strange monstrous shapes between the trees.

'Yes! Remember. It was by the wall just to the north of the farmhouse, lying there. The flies had started.'

The flies had started. A memory triggered. An image. Maggots crawling over blank eyes. A swollen, black tongue lolling from a broken jaw. Blood and pus clustered everywhere, maggots on that too. The whole thing writhing and wriggling. The stench. The prosecutor had later ruled that a neighbouring farmer had poisoned the cow to reduce the Nutters' profits.

'You do remember,' James said. He sounded relieved.

'What of it?' Alizon shrugged.

'You are as stupid as a newborn. Think about the cow, and now look at John. Do they look the same?'

Alizon gave him a hard look, then turned to John. Of course, there were no maggots. No blood, no pus. She opened John's mouth gently with her finger – no swollen black tongue.

Alizon raised her shoulders again. 'A different poison then? I am sure there is more than one.'

'Sister.' James's voice was calm now, soft, another trick. 'I have gone to many places, seen many things. I even spent a year on a ship, I have seen different islands and different shores. I have seen bodies, many of them. Illness or brutal murder or old age. You can tell straight away the cause, for most of them. I've only seen one other body that looks like this.' James paused, his eyes far away.

'It was in a place called Leeds, north from here. You have heard of it. It's where the road leads to. I was there for... well, it doesn't matter. But I met a girl. Gorgeous, she was. Blonde curls like nothing I've ever seen. And her laugh! Oh, she was lovely. I was courting her for a little while, in my way.' He smiled wistfully. 'But she wasn't interested, not really. Yes, she laughed and she flirted, but she could have married a lord. But then, I did something stupid. I upset somebody who shouldn't have been upset. And that somebody went for the only thing she knew was dear to me. By the time I realised what she was going to do, it was too late. I ran to my girl's lodgings, and there she was on her bed. Still, perfect, no sign of injury. But absolutely dead.' James finished his monologue and looked at Alizon.

She almost believed him.

'If you expect me to take your word, you need to tell me what you did.'

James squirmed uncomfortably. He looked embarrassed. 'Same as I always do.'

Alizon just looked.

'I came across a wise woman. That's what people named her, but I saw her for what she was. A witch. Just like Old Annie, she was.'

Alizon gasped. The word 'witch' wasn't thrown around so easily in Pendle, and although children sometimes shouted it at her and her family, no one ever said it of Old Annie.

'It's what she is. This woman, I saw her and I knew. I thought she would have some treasure in her house, just like Old Annie did that time. So I broke in. I had a good rifle through, took a few things, there was nothing too valuable there, but then I heard a noise. She was in the doorway. I pushed past her and ran, I hoped she hadn't seen my face, but of course she had. That was it. The witch killed my girl, as revenge.'

'So you think... you think John's death was

caused by witchcraft? You think Old Annie…? Because we stole the skull? Why would she have waited all of this time for her revenge?'

'No,' James said firmly, with exasperation in his voice, 'I've told you. This' – he gestured at John – 'was not Old Annie. This was our family.'

For the first time, Alizon understood what James was trying to say. It started with an uncomfortable nudge in the small of her back, then grew like a weed up her spine into her brain, where it pounded against her skull. John had left the village to visit Malkin Tower. What if they had recoiled against the idea of Alizon, their labour, leaving? What if they had offered him a drink, and he had accepted?

James must have seen the thought process written on Alizon's face, and his shoulders dropped. 'Yes, you see?'

Alizon took a few moments to reply. She had been so certain that James had done it. She thought of her family, the women she had lived with for her whole life.

'Old Demdike wouldn't,' Alizon said.

'You're the only one who looks after her. Losing you would be losing a lifeline,' James said.

'My mother wouldn't care; she is so distracted with our sister.'

'Losing you would mean she has to care for Old Demdike and our sister. The only body in the household who can work and gather food. You think she would choose that life?'

'Our sister is just a child.'

'Our sister is no ordinary child.'

Alizon fell silent. It was dusk, and getting cold. She shivered. She touched John's face. He was cold now, too. However much she tried, she couldn't marry the idea of the people she lived with murdering the man she loved. But then, according to James, he had never loved her. It was wrong. All wrong. Upside down.

James sat watching her. He was leaning back on his heels, his face grim.

'Which one do you think it was?'

'Who can say. Maybe all of them?' he said.

The trees rustled and swayed as a breeze picked up. Alizon wrapped her arms tightly around herself. 'But Jennet is so young. What did you mean when you said Jennet isn't an ordinary child?'

'You know what I mean. I have seen her only

briefly, and she makes me feel strange. I don't like it. She is different.'

'A five-year-old couldn't murder a man.'

'She could if the Devil led her.'

They fell into silence again. Alizon was thinking of that conversation after Jennet was born, when Old Demdike had said so clearly that she was one of them. *We'll go straight to Hell when we pass, girl, and I wouldn't be surprised if you do, too. Your blood is the same. You're one of us, whether you like it or not.*

With pain in her heart, Alizon recalled what she had said to James, what she had accused him of. 'James, I am so sorry for accusing you. Will you forgive me?'

James just shook his head, and Alizon wasn't sure whether he was refusing the apology or saying it was unnecessary.

'What do we do?' she asked, talking to herself as much as to her brother. The darkness was deepening, but when Alizon glanced down she saw John's skin had a sickly pearl glow, ice white.

James furrowed his brow. 'This could be our opportunity. All over the country, witches are being caught and sent to trial. There are special prosecutors who do it. Word is that the king himself was bewitched and now he is more serious than ever about stamping them out. We could report them, and they would...'

'James, no!'

'Look at what they did! They will do it again! Do you think you will ever be allowed to leave?' James was staring at her again, horror in his eyes.

'James,' Alizon said calmly. She knew what she needed to do. 'It's not that. I will never be allowed to leave, whatever happens. We can't tell anyone, because we will be blamed too. Who was John last seen with? Me, and you.'

James sighed heavily, and nodded. 'So what do you suggest we do?'

Alizon felt almost peaceful now. John was dead, but she had much bigger problems. There was a power over her, she knew it. She could never be rid of it. She had been foolish to think she could. 'We need to bury John, so no one will find him,' she said finally. 'I only hope he finds his way to Heaven. Then I must go back to the Tower so that no one else gets hurt.'

'You jest. You can't go back there. You know what they've done!'

'If I don't, they will find me anyway. If I do,

then I will be the only one to suffer. You can go. You can do as you wish. They don't seem to need you.'

Now it was James's turn to silently shake his head. Eventually, he roused himself to help Alizon dig a grave for John. Outside a churchyard though; they both knew he had no chance of reaching Heaven. At least it wasn't somewhere busy, where the footfall would trample him to the darkest depths. Darkness deepened and their breath began to mist in front of them as they laboured. After an hour of silent digging, together they rolled John into the hole. Alizon wished him a silent farewell with her eyes, then they began covering him with earth. When the hole was almost full, Alizon halted James, then pulled up a small sycamore sapling and placed it in the centre of the grave.

'This way, I will always know where he is, and I will always be able to visit him.' Alizon gently patted the sapling into place. James nodded and filled in the rest of the grave.

Darkness had fallen completely now. A thick, starless night. Alizon knew it was time to leave. She stood, every fibre of her body fighting against returning to that place. She rose against it.

'Where will you go?' she asked James.

'I'll be nearby,' James replied. 'If you're not leaving, then I'll be around, keeping an eye. I'm anxious for you.'

His eyes had lost their brightness. He looked much older than his eighteen years.

Alizon nodded slowly. Thought about how meaningless his protection really was. 'Thank you.' Then she turned her back on the grave, her chance of freedom dead, and walked down the hill.

11

Growing, growing,
  Roots holding deep,
  The mistletoe winds,
  Suffocates the host.

1610

Alizon sat stiffly on a stool, next to Old Demdike's ancient, worn chair. Her limbs were weary. She was only eighteen years old, but she felt a thousand. The first frosts had come, and they were always the worst. The icy realisation that the blankets and cloaks from the year before were destroyed by moths or just poor storage. The glances at the woodpile and the food stores, knowing they would never last through the winter.

She had spent the day up in the forest, looking

often at that growing sycamore, which she would never chop down for timber. She knew the wood she collected would never be enough. Those still, marble ice days in February would be fireless regardless.

But tonight, they sat before the fire.

'Well lit, Alizon. This fire dances,' Old Demdike muttered.

Alizon didn't reply. For over a year, she had spoken as little as possible. She watched, she saw, she was usually mute.

Old Demdike leaned forward, old bones creaking. 'Look at the stories it tells! We will become eminent, wealthy and fat it must mean! We will all leave this place, to go somewhere larger, much more impressive…' She paused, frowned at the patterns in the fire, then abruptly leaned back in her chair, silent.

Alizon ignored her. Old Demdike saw things in the fire most days. It never made any sense. The days, busy and away working, were manageable, but evenings were inescapable.

The sound Alizon had been dreading came. The door creaking open. Her mother and sister returning home.

Jennet ran in first. She perched directly in front of the fire, her back to the flames, facing Alizon and staring straight into her eyes. She began to sing, smiling all the time.

'Take a key key and lock padlock her up,
Lock padlock her up, lock padlock her up,
Take a key key and lock padlock her up,
My fair lady.'

Alizon drew herself in, shivering, but Elizabeth, stepping through the door, chuckled.

'The children at the well taught it to her. Doesn't she have the most perfect voice?'

There was no answer from Old Demdike or Alizon. Elizabeth shrugged. Jennet began again:

'Take a key key and lock padlock her up,
Lock padlock her up, lock padlock her up—'

'I am not hungry. Good night.' Alizon stood abruptly. She avoided everyone's eyes as she stepped through to the second room. She would not eat tonight, but it was worth it to enjoy a few more minutes away from her sister and mother, who shared the room with her.

She lay on her bed of straw, and as she did every night when she thought she wouldn't be seen, she pulled Night from under the straw. Her one memento of that sweet day. Her one, single possession. She kissed Night's head, turned him over and over, then thrust him back under the straw. She couldn't risk falling asleep with him visible in her hands.

It was cold, icy cold, and her blanket was thin. She kept all of her clothes on, but she still shivered and thought longingly of the fire in the other room. But this was better than sitting in there with them. Eventually, she fell into a fitful sleep.

That night, she dreamed of demons and broken flesh, dancing devils and weeping wounds. As always, just before she awoke, she saw blank, shallow eyes, staring into her soul.

When she woke she was sweating despite the cold. It was still dark, but the calls of the last birds preparing to leave told her that it was almost morning. Almost morning meant almost time to leave the Tower to work, and that was something to look forward to.

Alizon spent a few more minutes lying on her straw. She examined Night. The wood, which had once been rough, was worn smooth by her fingers. Every night, she rubbed and bothered Night with her fingers. It comforted her to know that she hadn't dreamed John, he wasn't part of her imagination, she really had once had a chance of escape, no matter if it had been all arranged by James.

She buried Night back underneath her straw

and rose from her bed. She glanced at her mother and Jennet, who shared a mound of straw across the room. Her mother was facing the opposite wall, and she was snoring loudly. Jennet was facing her and Alizon jumped when she saw her sister's open, staring eyes, before she realised that she was, as she so often did, sleeping with her eyes open.

Alizon crept through into the main room. Old Demdike was in her chair before the fireplace, also snoring, but much more softly than her daughter. As quietly as she could, without waking her grandmother, Alizon cleared the remnants of the previous day's fire and lit a new one. Old Demdike liked to wake in the warm.

Then, Alizon took a basket and ragged cloak and left the Tower before anyone else woke up.

Her days followed a seasonal routine now. She stayed away from the house and instead kept to the forest, gathering firewood, berries, mushrooms, wild garlic and anything else edible. She made rabbit traps and carefully hid them, mindful of the punishment for poachers if one of the lord's men (whose land this was) happened to pass this way. As it was, it was a dingy piece of land infrequently visited, which suited Alizon well. Alizon remembered her father's careful lessons about finding safe food: which mushrooms to avoid and where to find the best, dry wood. Those days, the sun always seemed to shine with golden light and James was always there, smiling and laughing.

As long as Alizon came back to the Tower with enough bounty, she avoided reprimand from her mother and grandmother. During the winter, it was even more important to make sure the rabbit traps were working well, otherwise they could go hungry. Some days, she needed to make repairs to the house, and whenever she did she imagined John laughing at her attempts at woodwork. The years that had passed had built a character for John in her mind, based on the few conversations they had. She secretly believed herself to be his widow.

Elizabeth, Jennet and Old Demdike spent their days very differently. Old Demdike, aged and ageless as ever, stayed by the fire. She rarely stood – Alizon barely knew if she could any more. She just watched the fire, and gave her wise words to villagers when Elizabeth led them to her.

Elizabeth and Jennet were becoming successful. They often came home with lumps of meat – a welcome addition for the stew pot, ale and mead. Alizon had seen from afar what they did. They would walk to the well, and wait there. Since Elizabeth had had Jennet, the villagers treated her with less hatred, though still as much, if not more, wariness. Eventually, one of the villagers would approach Elizabeth, always making sure no one was around first. They would whisper to Elizabeth, an exchange would take place, and some grim nodding. Occasionally, Elizabeth would take them to Malkin Tower to talk with Old Demdike, but only very rarely. Most often, this exchange would be all the contact they had, until sometime later – maybe a day or two, maybe weeks, sometimes months – the same villager would approach Elizabeth again with another gift. On one occasion, when all the talk in the village was about the unfortunate death of Henry Mitton, Elizabeth was given a whole cow, butchered. It lasted them for months.

Alizon couldn't put her finger on what it was about Jennet that made the villagers treat Elizabeth differently. She supposed it was probably because Jennet was a comely girl; the villagers felt sorry for her. Perhaps. Alizon thought she was strange. Off. Odd. She had never shaken those words James had said about her, that awful day in the woods. *She makes me feel strange. I don't like it. She is different.* And he had barely seen Jennet. There was just something different about her. She always watched, and she seemed to see your soul.

Of course, she was just a child, but she didn't talk to them as another person might talk. Instead, she would occasionally drop a phrase or a monologue into a room and leave everyone feeling deeply uncomfortable. For example, there had been the time when Old Demdike had been treating them to a story about her life in Whalley when she was a child, and Jennet began laughing hysterically when Old Demdike was describing her own mother. When Elizabeth had asked why she was laughing, Jennet had just replied, 'Split like a plum!'

They weren't words Old Demdike had spoken, and Elizabeth had looked confused, but Old Demdike's face had turned grey and she began to tremble. She refused to tell stories about her childhood after that.

There were other things too. The way she hummed: a low humming which you didn't notice at first, until it built and you thought you were going mad. Then she would stop suddenly, and you would realise what she had been doing. A childish game, perhaps, but it always seemed like there was more to it than that.

Then, there was the night Alizon had returned

after John's death. Elizabeth had screamed at her, called her 'whore' and 'slut'; Old Demdike had looked disapproving too. Alizon hadn't explained what had happened, and it quickly became clear that John had never reached the Tower. Alizon had felt numb and scared, wondering which of them had planned it, which of them had carried it out. Then she caught Jennet's eyes. She had been sitting in front of the fire, playing with something. Jennet held up what she had been playing with. A doll. Alizon had never seen it before. She took it. It was shaped like a man, and made of wood. Thinking of John's profession, she thrust the doll back at Jennet, who had slowly, carefully, placed it in the centre of the fire, staring into Alizon's eyes the whole time. Alizon stared at the burning man, and it must have been her grief and her tiredness, but as the flames licked at him, the doll looked more and more like John, screaming. Alizon had run from the room then, ignoring the shouts that followed her. To this day, Alizon felt a shiver when she recalled that night. It made her uncomfortable to think about where the doll might have come from.

Still, Jennet was a child and it was ridiculous to fear her. She was seven years old; she had been five when John died. James had been wrong to think she had anything to do with it. Surely. Elizabeth was the most likely culprit. Alizon wished she had the courage to tell them what she thought she knew.

James. She wished she could talk to him today. He had stayed around the local area after John's death, but he rarely made himself visible to Alizon. She spotted him every now and then, but whenever she hurried towards him he melted into thin air. He clearly didn't want to talk to her after what had happened to his friend. She could understand why, after everything she had accused him of, but she wished he would forgive her.

On this particular day, as Alizon reached the point where Malkin Tower just began to disappear out of view, she heard a shout behind her. Sighing, she turned and saw Elizabeth waving at her. She headed back to the Tower.

'Go to the village. If there is a pedlar I need small glass bottles. Take this.' Elizabeth pressed a coin into Alizon's hand. 'You come back with the bottles or the coin. Otherwise the Devil won't be able to save you.'

Alizon nodded and turned again. This was the usual interaction she expected from her mother. She was brisk, abrupt, unkind. She had been since she had a new daughter to lavish with her love.

So, Alizon wandered towards the village. She was in no hurry, had no friends there. She hoped that there would be a pedlar set up on the closest edge of the village, so that she could get the job done and still have some time to spend in the forest on the way back.

As she walked, Alizon felt the filth of the house flow off her. Even though the house was not really dirty – she kept it better than it had ever been kept before – it felt grim and dusty. There was something about it that would never be clean. She dreamed of the day when the earth consumed it.

It was another cold day, but bright; the frost was melting in the places where the sun's fingers reached. It was pleasant to walk along, listening to the silence.

All too soon, Alizon reached the outer edge of the village. The first cluster of houses were large; they got smaller towards the centre of the village. It was quiet, it was still early, but there were a few people milling around. A child was playing in front of one of the houses, next to its mother who was beating some washing. The child tripped, fell, as Alizon walked past and the mother immediately scooped it up, shushing and rocking to quell its cries. Alizon averted her eyes and increased her pace.

Towards the centre of the village, there were lots of people around. Alizon was relieved to see a pedlar in the middle of them, and made her way over. She tried not to notice the villagers stepping away from her, but it did hurt. She hadn't cared about her appearance for a long time, spending her days either in the forest or at the Tower, and she suddenly became aware of her tangled, filthy hair, her ragged clothes, her dirty skin. When had she last washed? She began to wish it was raining, rather than this bright sunshine highlighting all of her many flaws.

She straightened herself upright and pushed towards the pedlar, avoiding everyone's eyes.

'Small glass bottles, please,' Alizon said, holding out her coin.

The pedlar frowned at her and said with a thick, unrecognisable accent, 'I've just sold all of my glass bottles. That woman there bought them.'

The pedlar pointed at a woman standing a few feet away. A woman of around fifty years old, who Alizon recognised with a jolt. Anne Redferne. Old Annie's daughter. She hadn't seen her for a couple of years.

Although Alizon tried to turn and leave quickly, Anne spotted her.

'Alizon Device? Elizabeth's girl?'

'Yes. I was here for bottles.' She kept her head bowed, didn't want to look directly at the woman she had stolen from once upon a time.

'Well, you're out of luck. I bought all of the bottles. But what would a girl like you be wanting with small bottles anyway?' Anne peered closely at Alizon.

'I... I was buying them for my mother. She asked me to. She needs them.' Something about Anne's question had made Alizon feel as though she had done something wrong.

'Your mother?' Anne asked. She seemed taken aback. 'Did she want them for Old Demdike?'

The questions were confusing Alizon. She couldn't work out why Anne would care. A hint of a feeling – the rumours about Old Annie and her daughter, about Old Demdike and her offspring. What was Anne trying to suggest? 'I don't know, she didn't say.'

A sudden, bright smile from Anne. A sudden, bright change of subject: 'And how are your mother and Old Demdike? Your brother and sister?'

'Fine, well.' Alizon could think of nothing else

to say about her family. 'How is Old Annie?' She couldn't remember whether Anne had any other relatives, a husband, children.

'She's well. Surviving. Almost completely blind now, can you imagine! But it doesn't stop her. I'm sure you understand. As far as I remember, she and Old Demdike are very alike.' She smiled widely, revealing a row of black teeth.

Alizon shuddered. Anne looked, waiting for a response perhaps.

When none came, Anne said, 'Well, I'm sorry about the bottles! Have a pleasant day.'

She turned to leave, and as she did so Alizon noticed the strange atmosphere in the square. The villagers were huddled in groups of two and three, muttering to one another, stopping when Alizon looked at them. Alizon shrugged, walked past them. As she did so, the muttering intensified and Alizon saw, she couldn't miss it, the hand gestures. Index finger against thumb. Protection from the evil eye. Protection from spells. Protection from witches. Alizon picked up her pace and ran from the village.

She ran and ran, pausing only when she reached the confines of the forest. And it was there that she realised that at some point during her flight, she

must have dropped the coin. No bottles, and no coin.
She sank to the floor, hands over her eyes, and wept.

12

Unfolding, thickening,
  Cultivating, maturing,
  Swelling, multiplying,
  Germinating, producing.

1611

Jennet was dancing in the garden. It was a garden now, not a barren wasteland as it had been for so many years. Alizon watched her from the log she was using as a seat. She had worked her fingers to the bone for the place. She spent every day weeding, planting, trimming and tying. She treated those plants and herbs as her babies; babies she knew she would never have in real life. She felt that, certain as she'd never been certain about anything, in her womb.

As Jennet danced, the herbs crushed under her

feet. The smell of rosemary, lavender and thyme floated into the air, mixed with the bumbling bees and drunk butterflies.

'Please stop, Jennet. You will kill the plants,' Alizon begged. She knew what would happen if the plants died. She flinched from the punishment. Her arm was still scarred from the whack with a burning log she had received that day she admitted losing the coin, and the multiple beatings she had received since then for who knows how many misdemeanours. Ever since she had returned that day everything she did was wrong. And every wrong thing resulted in a beating.

Jennet laughed, and carried on dancing. Part of Alizon felt jealous of the joy; how long had it been since she had felt the bliss in a warm summer's day?

Alizon watched blankly as the plants were trampled, trampled under the rotating girl.

'Alizon!' A deep voice.

Alizon flinched.

'Alizon! You shouldn't let her do that!'

Elizabeth stormed towards her. She was carrying a lot of weight now, and the wrinkles growing on her face accentuated the lopsided eyes. She might have looked fine, healthy at least, had it not been for her habitual angry grimace.

This was typical of Elizabeth. If Jennet did something wrong, it was anyone's fault but Jennet's. Jennet could do no wrong in Elizabeth's eyes. Jennet smiled widely and Elizabeth's face softened. 'Come, chick,' she cooed, 'time to go to the well.'

Jennet chuckled and hugged her mother, who squeezed her back, and the two walked off without a glance back at Alizon.

Alizon sighed heavily. Life was getting worse and worse for her. No way out. She was treated worse than a slave, expected to carry out all of the jobs around the house while Elizabeth and Jennet did as they wished. Old Demdike had gone blind overnight, the day Alizon had seen Anne Redferne in the village, just like Old Annie had (the very same day, so they said), so caring for her took even more time too.

Alizon had begun to spend her nights sleeping on the straw and holding Night, dreaming of her family's downfall or her escape. Many nights, she dreamed of just walking off one morning and never stopping, keeping on going, until she was somewhere else. But she was too scared. There were so few options for a girl her age. And always bearing down on her was the fear for her soul; she wasn't sure if it was God or the Devil that she feared the most. Other nights, she dreamed of darker things. Knives and axes and shards of broken glass. The hatred and bile that she kept hidden during the day rose up in her nightmares, the corpses of her family around her.

She was reaching breaking point, she could feel it in the tension in her skull. She had started to believe that her decision to stay at Malkin Tower after John's death hadn't been her choice, that she had been tricked into it somehow. She refused to believe that she would have given up her chance at freedom so easily. She felt frustrated and angry. And every night, that anger turned to blood in her dreams.

She wished she had James's mind. He would be able to see a way out of this mess. He would know. But James hadn't been around for a long time. He was keeping his distance, and Alizon didn't know how to find him.

Alizon stood up and turned. Screaming, she leaped back and tripped over the log, ending up prostrate on the ground. Old Demdike had been standing right in front of her, inches away.

Shaken, Alizon lifted herself up. 'Why are you outside?' she asked.

Old Demdike turned her milky white eyes in

her direction. 'I could feel dread,' she said strongly. 'You need to do something.'

Had Old Demdike read her mind? Did she know about the dreams? Alizon led Old Demdike back inside, into her chair. As always, the fire was lit, even though it was warm outside. Alizon perched on the stool next to the fire.

'What do you mean?' she asked finally.

Old Demdike did not answer for a few moments. Her jaw was working, as though she was chewing. Alizon looked closely at her. Her almost hairless head was covered with marks and moles, and a large mole had grown on the left side of her nose, too. The cloudy eyes were sunken, shadows in a skull.

Just when Alizon thought that Old Demdike would not answer at all, she began to talk.

'Something is coming, child. I can feel it.'

'What is coming?' Normally, Alizon would have ignored her words, but today it felt different.

'The cold. The dark. The end.'

In a rush of sympathy, Alizon wrapped her own warm hands around Old Demdike's icy ones. She must be foreseeing her own death. Alizon had heard of old people doing this before; it was well known that once you lived to a certain age, you might see the end. Usually, God-fearing folk might catch a glimpse of Heaven, but Old Demdike didn't sound as though she had seen that.

'What do you see?' Alizon asked tremulously.

'The cold. The dark. The end,' Old Demdike said again, in the same dull tone.

Alizon waited. She could not believe that Old Demdike would have gone to the effort of rising to her chair and feeling her way to the garden to tell her this. There must be something more urgent.

Alizon had no idea how much time passed, sitting in the stifling heat beside the flickering fire, before Old Demdike spoke again.

'The darkness is coming, and you need to make a choice,' Old Demdike said suddenly. 'There is darkness coming. You thrust away your mother and sister, but could they be the ones to save you?'

'What do you mean?' It made Alizon anxious to hear that Old Demdike knew about her feelings towards Elizabeth and Jennet. Perhaps she told them, when Alizon had gone to bed.

'I mean that the darkness is coming, aren't you listening girl?' Old Demdike leaned forward, her voice had become urgent. 'The darkness is coming and if I were younger, I would be looking to your sister to save me. What will you do?'

Shortly after delivering these words, Old Demdike tipped her head back and began to snore.

Alizon felt all of her tension release and she began to laugh at herself. The thought that she had got so worked up, and Old Demdike had been sleepwalking and dreaming! She stood and walked back out into the sunshine, feeling a renewed energy. The day was young, her sister and mother might be gone for hours, and Old Demdike was asleep. She could work on her garden in peace.

She started by trying to repair those plants which had been trampled. The rosemary was easily remedied, as was the thyme, but the lavender was crushed. It would need water and time, but Alizon didn't want to visit the well. Villagers would be there. Perhaps her mother would come back with some water.

Then, she moved on to the weeding. Although her back creaked, Alizon felt healthy and strong. Her shoulders and arms were well muscled from the gardening, her legs thick from walking. She was still young, she thought, though she was starting to lose count of the years, and, on that sunny day, with the warmth tickling her bones, she let herself daydream about someone finding her attractive. Someone enjoying her, her enjoying someone. A well-hidden memory rose up, filled her with longing. She worked harder.

The sun followed its arc, and Alizon worked. When the sun just began its dip, Alizon heard laughter echoing and knew that her mother and Jennet were drawing closer. For some reason, and she couldn't quite fathom why, she wasn't filled with dread as she usually was. She just carried on. And when Elizabeth yelled that the food needed cooking, she just shrugged and brushed her hands, walked into the house and busied herself with the cooking pot. There was stew, and Elizabeth and Jennet had come back with bread. A feast.

Elizabeth was looking at her oddly; she had noticed the change in behaviour, but Alizon didn't care. She filtered through her feelings to try to work out the change in her mother, but she couldn't. She didn't know.

'Alizon. We need thyme. Pick a large bunch,' Elizabeth ordered.

Alizon nodded, collected the thyme from her garden and passed it to Elizabeth.

Elizabeth peered at her blank expression. 'And a lock of your hair.'

'My… my hair?' Alizon's confidence from earlier in the day fell from her as though it had never existed. Why would her mother want a lock of her hair? What would she do with it? Nothing good ever came from handing over a lock of hair. There was one thing it pointed to. Witchcraft. Spells. Dark magic.

'Yes. Cut some and give it to me.'

'But, I, no…' Alizon took some involuntary steps backwards.

Elizabeth shook her head slightly. 'You give it to me, or I will take it.'

Jennet let out a shred of laughter.

Alizon shuddered. 'Why?' she asked.

Somehow, Elizabeth and Jennet were between Alizon and the door. She wouldn't be able to get past them in this cramped space. Old Demdike was behind her, and so was the door leading through to the bedroom. That wouldn't help, though.

'Just give it to me.'

Elizabeth's face was becoming flushed. Anger at the non-acquiescence. Alizon was so trampled underfoot that she would do anything she was told in order to survive. But for some reason, not today.

Alizon began edging slowly backwards, her heart thumping in her chest. She might be able to fight them off with the wall behind her, to lean on. If she fought them off for long enough, then maybe they would tire and... Her plan would not finish itself. She was becoming panicked. She didn't want to be a part of whatever they were doing.

'You give me your hair, or I will take it from your bleeding corpse,' Elizabeth growled. An empty threat, surely.

With a jolt, Alizon saw that Elizabeth was now holding a long, jagged knife. She had never seen this knife before. Her mother's eyes were dark and heavy, and, for the first time, something inside Alizon told her that this was not a shallow threat. Elizabeth would kill her if she had to. Her mother clearly had her reasons for needing to carry out this curse, and Alizon suspected she had been threatened. This must be why she was so aggressive.

Acid rose in Alizon's throat as she weighed up her options. She could fight, try to run, but likely die in the process. Or, she could hand over her hair. Doing so would mean knowingly taking part in witchcraft, and that meant giving up any chance she had of God's forgiveness.

She was deeply afraid, but in that moment she knew she was too much of a coward to give her life now. Tears began to roll down her face as she felt the dirt of the wall under her fingers. Without raising her eyes to her mother's, she pulled her hair out of their braids and held a lock towards her mother, who hacked it roughly with her knife. She tugged, and it hurt, which made Alizon sob more. She was trying to do it as quickly as possible. When it was done, Alizon dropped down to sitting on the floor. She felt as though her guts were made from heavy iron, her head in a vice. She had just guaranteed herself eternal damnation. That was what the Church would say. Her soul would live in Hell. And all because she was too afraid of pain. She was worthless. Nothing. Her life was over.

Through the depths of her despair, Alizon heard a crack and sizzle, and an acrid smell told her unmistakably that her hair was burning in the fire. She clenched her eyes tightly shut. She didn't want to see what was happening in the room. She wrapped her arms around her, raised knees and buried her head between them, trying to drown out what sounded like Jennet's laughter.

It felt like hours. She stayed still, unmoving,

trying to ignore her family. Some part of her felt that if she didn't witness what happened, maybe she would be spared when judgement day came. Maybe.

There was a prodding in her side. She opened her eyes, peered sideways. Her sister. Smiling widely, madly, staring at her. Alizon shuddered and heaved herself to her feet. She shielded her eyes from the rest of the room and shuffled through to the bedroom.

She rifled through her straw to find Night. Her anchor, her comfort. She curled up in the straw feeling utterly bereft.

As a child, Alizon had always feared God. Her father had been a Christian man, and he had taken her to church. The pastor had been terrifying to a young child. Thin as a skeleton, his pasty, white skin stretched over his skull. His mouth was a black cavern and he would thrash his words down to the congregation. Lots of what he had said had been too difficult for Alizon to understand: he talked of kings and queens Alizon had barely heard of as though they were his personal friends; he reeled off stories from his huge Bible and the men blurred together – the Jacobs and the Davids and the Samuels.

But when he spoke of witchcraft, it was different. His passion rose and he would smash the lectern with his fist. The king had told him, the king had told him, that witches were condemned to Hell, and the king was the voice of God on earth. One day, he had walked down the aisle brandishing a book as though he was its proud father. *Daemonologie*, he had shouted, written by King James, our saviour! Alizon remembered shrinking away from the book as though it was the king himself. Our brave and learned king has blessed us with knowledge, the pastor had explained excitedly. He has been so kind as to give us the tools to recognise and smite down witchcraft! The Devil works in many ways, but none so much as through the words of witches! If you are offered a spell, or a potion, if someone promises revenge for you or to rid you of your enemies, if someone claims to cure you of your ills, when you know they are not a doctor, that person is a witch and it is your duty (here he began to spit each word, his excitement was so great), your duty to your king and therefore your God to tell me of this person and allow God's justice to be served!

Here he had paused, his bulging eyes passing over the congregation. Alizon had noticed that most of them were shifting uneasily; it would be hard to find anyone in the area who had not gone to a wise woman for a cure rather than a doctor. Doctors were too expensive for most people to afford, whereas a wise woman might cure you for some grain or meat. But Alizon also knew there were many in the audience who had used spells or potions. She knew because – and here she glanced sideways at her father, who was staring forward, unconcerned – she had heard whispers at Malkin Tower.

The pastor had noticed the bristling and smiled a slow, sardonic smile. Furthermore! He had shouted, a fist punching the air. Anyone found to be associating with witches, assisting witches or shielding witches will also be subject to God's judgement! And it is clear – here his voice lowered, became a purr – quite clear, that God's judgement in the case of witches is eternal damnation. An eternity of pain and labour in Hell.

The pastor's fevered speech and the ones that followed may have put some off approaching wise women, but most carried on with their life as normal. The only thing that changed was the accusation of witchcraft – previously thrown around as a petty insult – now became a threat. If the authorities heard the accusation, you could end up on the gallows.

But for Alizon, those words stuck with her. She thought now about whether she had been wilfully blind about her family's acts, and she knew that ever since that conversation with Old Demdike and Elizabeth, after Jennet was born, that she could be accused of assisting witches. But she had never, until today, taken part in witchcraft. Her decision had condemned her. Before, perhaps, God may have pitied her. Now, she would be cast into Hell. Even if she told the pastor now about her family, she couldn't be saved. She clutched Night tightly.

There were only two things she could do, she thought. She could run away, run away from Malkin Tower as she had considered so many times in the past. Make a new life for herself. Maybe she could do enough good to persuade God that it had been a mistake. But where would she go? She had nothing. She knew the opportunities were scarce, she had no family or friends to support her. Where would she even go?

Her second option was to get on with her life at the Tower. If they worked hard, they might live comfortably. Old Demdike was over eighty years old; Alizon could have years and years before she would have to face her judgement. And if Alizon accepted who her family were, did what they wanted her to do, well, perhaps life might be easier for her.

Although the spectre of the Devil leered over her still, Alizon felt comforted by the years that separated them. She just needed to survive. And the longer she survived, the better. She managed to drift into sleep, into strange dreams full of shadows and screaming men.

13

Death, my friend
  You draw near
  Wrap me in
  Your embrace

1612

Elizabeth had been very clear. They needed pins. The pins were necessary for the work, and without them they would not be paid. So pins were what Alizon would get.

She walked into the village, the walk shortened by her strong strides, and approached a pedlar. There was only one today, and he had no pins.

'Beardshaw is where you need to go,' the pedlar said. 'I've just been there.'

Beardshaw was the next village along. Not a

very long walk, and it was a bright and warm March day, so Alizon nodded her thanks and set on her way. It was morning still, and she had the whole day ahead of her. Morning was always her favourite time of day. She walked slowly, revelling in the scents and scenes of springtime. It had been a long winter, and this was the first properly warm day in so many months. She would take the time to enjoy this stroll.

To get to Beardshaw, the quickest route was through Trawden Forest. The path was well trodden, and bluebells were poking up on either side of the path. The birds were busy and Alizon's dress was making a pleasing swishing sound on the ground as she walked. It was still an unfamiliar feeling for her, but she felt happy.

Life at the Tower, as she had predicted, became easier when she began to offer her help more actively. Elizabeth had even begun to teach Alizon some of her skills. 'Thyme for a storm, daughter, rosemary for a birth, bay for a bounty,' she would say, reeling off herbs and their magical properties. Much of what she did was curing villagers of their trivial complaints: a rotten toenail, a broken tooth, a rash. The pins were for Samuel Cartwright's warts, and he had promised to pay well. Now that Alizon knew some of the secrets, she felt less worried. Her memories of the pastor seemed a long way away now, and what could be the harm in curing villagers? Of course, there were the occasional jobs which were… different, but Old Demdike and Elizabeth tended to do those together, and for the moment Alizon was happy not to get involved.

As Alizon walked, she hummed. She had a high-pitched voice still, like a young girl's, and she liked the sound mixing with the chirping birds as she walked.

The trees were close on either side, and the path became narrow. As she walked, she began to hear an echo, mirroring her own footsteps. She paused, stopped singing and listened closely. Yes – footsteps.

It was not always safe for a woman to walk alone through the forest, and so Alizon stepped off the path and into the shadows of the trees. Because the trees pressed in so much at this part of the path, it was some time before the owner of the footsteps came into view. Gradually, an outline became a man, and as he came closer the details became clearer. When he was almost past her, Alizon noticed he had the pack of a pedlar. She decided to break cover.

'Wait!' she cried.

The pedlar jumped and whipped round to face her, his face drained of colour. He looked terrified.

'I'm sorry to give you a fright.' Alizon smiled. 'I was wondering if I might have some pins?'

The man frowned at her; the colour had not returned to his face. 'No money, no pins,' he said.

'Oh, I have some money, I'm Alizon Device from Malkin Tower, we're not beggars,' Alizon began, but the man shook his head and restarted his trudging walk.

'No, stop!' Alizon said. She rifled in her skirts for the money but could not find it quickly enough, and the man was walking away. She ran the few yards after him and grabbed his arm. He shook her off.

'Get away from me, beggar, thief!' he yelled.

'I'm no thief!' she replied, still rifling in her pockets. This man could cause her to fall out of favour with her family, to lose the payment from Samuel Cartwright. She pulled out Night, who she had taken to carrying around everywhere, and held him in her left hand while she continued searching for her money bag. She finally grasped it, pulled it out and thrust it into the pedlar's face. 'See!' She waved the money bag.

But the pedlar was not looking at the money bag. He was pale still, unnaturally pale, and now he was beginning to shake. Wordlessly, he pointed at Night and then at Alizon's face.

Alizon was confused, couldn't understand what the man was doing. She just wanted the pins, and this stupid man wasn't doing what she wanted. He was frustrating her, with his strange, weepy eyes and his funny mouth. 'Why don't you just give me the pins?'

The pedlar was trying to get some words out. His jaw was working, round and round, like he was chewing. 'F— f— familiar!' He was pointing at Night again. 'Y— you! W— witch!'

The words made Alizon angrier still. Did he know how dangerous they were? He was calling her a witch because she had a wooden dog? She could hit him. She wanted to hit him with Night, pound the stupid man with him until his skull was crushed and bloody. Stupid. Stupid. Why didn't he just give her the pins? She began to pull at his pack, she would just take the pins. She was angrier than she had ever been. She felt Night hot in her hand with the electricity of her fury. As she pulled at the pack, the pedlar desperately batting her away, her hand brushed the man's face. As it did, something very strange happened.

The man froze. His whole body. Alizon let go of the pack, curious. Was this some trick? The man's jaw went slack, the skin around his eyes too. His eyes, though – his eyes looked like a caught rabbit's, the whites showing, staring this way and that. His arms dropped to his sides and his legs collapsed underneath him. He lay on the ground, all awkward angles, looking like a dead man. But those eyes, those eyes stared up at her still. Fearful.

His jaw was working, chewing, drool beginning to pool on the left side and overflow. As Alizon began to realise that this was not a trick, and wonder if she should get somebody to help, a word managed to escape. Slurred and drunk, but unmistakable.

'Witch.'

Night was still in her left hand, and he was as hot as embers. She felt the remnants of the fury rolling off her, and as she stared down at the man, panic began to take its place.

Had she caused this? She had wished him ill, and look what had happened... he was prostrate, frozen, but those eyes... he looked... he looked as though he had been cursed. Alizon glanced around frantically. No one was there. What could she do? What should she do?

She looked down at Night, still burning hot, and dropped him. What had she done? What had she summoned? She had done something terrible, she felt it like a rock in her stomach. Helping her family with those little spells had seemed harmless, but now, now it seemed something much, much greater had happened.

Her fingers fluttered over him, but he just lay there with those eyes and that spittle and those strangely angled legs (a mirror of her last image of John... she forced the memory down) and those eyes, staring, knowing, watching, fearing. Seeing no other option, Alizon swiftly got to her feet and ran, ran like the beasts of Hell were snapping at her feet (or doing her bidding?) until she reached home.

She entered the house trembling like a leaf, pale and grey. Elizabeth stopped what she was doing and rushed over to her.

'What on earth has happened?' she asked.

Alizon just shook her head, her legs collapsed underneath her and she fell to the floor.

'Are you ill?' Her mother gently felt her forehead and Alizon, unused to this treatment, closed her eyes slowly.

'Here.' Elizabeth pulled Alizon to her feet and led her through to the bedroom, lying her carefully on the bed. Alizon knew that her appearance must have seriously shocked her mother, because she hadn't even mentioned the pins.

Elizabeth gave Alizon a spiced tincture, which she drank without complaint. She gratefully allowed her mother to let her sleep.

Alizon spent the next few days going over and over what had happened. She felt bone achingly guilty, and often battled with herself about whether to go back to the forest and find him. She imagined him lying there still, frozen but alive, slowly dying of thirst and able to do nothing. But if she was found with him...

She also realised that at some point during the altercation, she had dropped Night. She mourned his presence, and desperately wanted to find him. She thought about telling Jennet, asking her to go and find Night, but if she came across the man... and she had managed to keep Night a secret from her family for such a long time, her one possession, she didn't want to share it now. She decided she would wait. In a few weeks, a month maybe, she would go back and find Night.

Alizon was terribly conflicted. She knew now that she had power, or certainly, she had power when she had Night. At times, she tried to see what else she could do, but nothing ever happened. She just didn't have the knowledge.

There was nothing else to link her to the man. If anyone else found Night, that wouldn't lead them to her... and she was sure no one had seen them entering the forest.

She slept badly, worrying about the man and about herself; whenever she dropped off for a few moments, a vision of the man's animalistic, petrified eyes appeared before her and she jerked awake. The lack of sleep was making her feel heavy and pulled tight, like a taut piece of string. She knew she looked tired too. It was helping to bolster Elizabeth's idea that she was ill.

With each day that went past, she knew, it was less likely that the man had survived. She felt the guilt like a rock chained to her leg. She pulled it around with her as she foggily carried out her daily chores. The man's face was there every time she blinked. She knew it would be for the rest of her life.

Three days after it happened, Alizon was listlessly weeding in the garden. Her muscles felt like sludge; everything was taking so much longer than it normally would. Her eyes were sore every time she blinked. She hoped that the monotonous, hard work would take her mind away, wear her out so that she could sleep tonight.

She leaned down, pulled, raised, leaned down, pulled, raised. An ache began to form in her back; it felt good, she carried on. Lean down, pull, raise. Lean down, pull, raise.

Elizabeth and Jennet were out, as was usual during the day. Old Demdike was indoors by the fire. Even the birds were quiet today.

A fly began to bother Alizon. It buzzed around her ears, disturbing her peace, breaking her rhythm. She batted it away, but it returned, the buzzing filling her head. She swatted and flung her arms around, trying to kill the nuisance. It kept coming back, its constant noise drilling into her. She paused, her eyes following the fly. Then clapped. She had caught it. It dropped to the floor; her peace returned. Alizon allowed herself a small smile, stretched and turned around to see a man standing behind her, a look of obvious disgust on his face.

Alizon gasped. Was it a ghost? A spectre?

'Alizon Device?' the man said in a gravelly voice. No ghost, then.

'Y… yes?' Alizon replied. She raised her frightened eyes to his. What was this person doing here?

He must have eased the front gate open and wandered down the path; the thought of him entering their land without permission made her frightened. He had a thick, dark beard and squinting eyes hidden under huge eyebrows. Somehow he looked familiar.

'My name is Abraham Law. I would like you to come with me.'

Abraham Law. The name meant nothing to Alizon. She had never even heard of a family of Laws. There weren't any in the village.

'Who are you?' she asked thickly. Maybe lack of sleep had made her slow.

'I have need of your skills,' the man answered.

Ah. This made sense. He wanted healing, or a spell.

'My grandmother is inside. Would you like to speak with her?' Alizon replied. With Elizabeth being away from the house, Old Demdike was the one who would be able to help.

'No,' the man replied brusquely. 'You're the one I need. Will you come with me?'

Alizon felt confused. She was not skilled; no one ever asked for her. No one would want to. How had he even got her name?

'I think you're mistaking me for somebody else. If you'll just come inside, my grandmother—'

'No!' Abraham interrupted. 'Listen. You are the one I need. You come with me, or I will drag you.'

The violence of his words shocked her. She felt cold, could see no way out. She had no father, no husband to protect her. She resolved that it would be less dangerous to go with him, do whatever job he wanted, and return home as soon as possible.

She nodded once. 'May I wash?' she asked, holding up her dirt-crusted hands.

'No time. Come.'

The man turned and walked down the path. Alizon shuddered and followed. In the back of her mind, she thought of that pedlar. Even though she didn't have Night, surely if the man tried to hurt her she could stop him. She wished she could have told Old Demdike that she was leaving. Maybe she had heard; her hearing was keener now that her sight had failed.

Round the crest of the hill, just out of sight of the house, they reached a horse and cart. The man must have left it here so that he could approach Malkin Tower without being noticed. The cart was enclosed, she had often seen farmers use these to take their goods to market: the covering protected anything inside from the rain.

Abraham opened the cart and gestured inside. 'Get in.'

Alizon hesitated. It was dark in there, and if she was inside she would not be able to see where they were going.

Anger and frustration were rising in Abraham's eyes. 'We have a way to go, and there is no room on the horse for you. You get in, or I swear it, I will tie you to the horse and you can run alongside.'

This was all the encouragement Alizon needed. She curled herself into the cart, the door was slammed behind her, and she felt the darkness cover her.

Alizon had only ever travelled by foot before, and the jolting of the cart felt strange and unsettling. It rocked over the path, up and down, up and down, Alizon's stomach rolling over and over each time. She heaved but, having not eaten much over the last few days, nothing came up.

The journey went on and on. In her dark box, Alizon had no idea how much time had passed, how far they were travelling. Where were they going? What was the point in Abraham taking her? She meant nothing. She always had. Worthless.

Just as the journey had begun to feel endless, the cart stopped. Alizon heard Abraham dismount the horse and tread towards her. There was the sound of wood on wood, a sliver of light, then, in a rush, the door was open and Alizon was blinking in the brightness.

Abraham grabbed her arm and pulled her from the cart. She swayed on her feet; her body was still recovering from the rocking.

She looked around. They were in front of a fairly large house, well kept. The road was well worn, and clearly used by horses and carts often. The house had fields behind it and woodland before it; no other houses were in view.

Abraham was busying himself with the horse. He freed it from its harness, then led it around the side of the house and out of sight.

Alizon allowed herself a moment to consider her options. She could run, now, but she had no idea where she was. He would likely find her in minutes, and then it would be even worse.

And then, before she had time to decide what

to do, Abraham was back and beckoning her into the house.

'What job do you want from me, sir?' Alizon asked, trying to sound confident. He didn't answer.

It was dark inside. Alizon could see though that it was well furnished and fairly richly decorated, with rugs on the floor. There was a dresser against a wall boasting beautifully decorated crockery.

Abraham led her through to a room at the back of the house. A fire was burning here, and candles were lit. There was a bed, with a comfortable-looking and rumpled bedcover. Alizon began to wonder exactly what it was that Abraham was expecting of her.

Then, the bedcover spoke. 'This is her?'

There was a small, withered man lying on the bed.

Abraham walked closer to the bed. 'Yes,' he replied. 'She came without too much issue.'

'Thank you,' the cracked, slurred little voice said. 'You had better stay. Witness. In case.'

Abraham nodded and moved over to a chair in the corner of the room, by the fire. There he sat, watching closely.

'Come closer, girl. I want you to see me,' the voice said.

Alizon moved closer. The man had a wispy, white beard and his eyes were sunken and bleary. He, too, looked vaguely familiar.

'My name is John Law,' the man said. 'I think you know me?'

'I think you must have brought the wrong person. I don't know you,' Alizon replied, though something was tugging on her memory.

'Yes, you do. I know you. You are Alizon Device.'

Alizon had to lean closer, the speech was difficult to understand. 'You gave me your name, though I didn't give you mine,' she heard him murmur.

Alizon peered at him. There was recognition. Definitely recognition. Who was he?

'I'm Alizon, but I don't know you. I will go now.' Alizon turned, and at the same time Abraham stood. He was big, and his bulk filled the room. Alizon began to panic.

'You will stay. You will see what you did to me.'

'What I...?' Could it be? How? How had he...?

'Ah. You do know me,' John slurred, and Alizon fell to her knees, grasping his hand.

'Forgive me, it was a mistake. I did not know... I regret it all.'

Abraham tutted. 'You need to cure him.'

Alizon looked up at him. 'I don't know how! I don't know what I did. I wished evil things; I just wanted the pins. I didn't mean to hurt him, but I did. I did.'

Abraham's face had gone ruddy with anger. He grabbed Alizon's hair and thrust her head forward, close to John's.

'You did not mean to?' he sneered. 'Look. Look at what you did! This is evil. Foul. Cure him, witch!'

Alizon began to sob. 'Please, John Law, I beg your forgiveness! I did not mean to. I never thought I had any power, but... then this happened. I don't know how to take it back.'

Before John could respond, Abraham shoved something into her face. 'If you thought you had no power,' he mocked, 'then why do you have a familiar?'

Alizon focused on Abraham's hand. There, he had it. It was Night. Alizon's stomach dropped. She remembered, word for word, what the pastor had said. And the most powerful of these foul witches, the most evil, shall be able to summon a familiar, a dog or a cat or some other animal, and that animal shall do their bidding. And if you meet this witch, it is your DUTY to God and to the king to bring them to justice. Save this earth from this pestilence.

'It's not… I didn't…' but even as she was stuttering these words, she thought back to that day. Night had grown hot, hadn't he? And when he had grown hot, that was when John fell… 'John Law! Please, I beg forgiveness. I have been led by evil, I have been seduced by the Devil, I wish with all my heart that this had never happened!'

'So you admit it?' Abraham asked gruffly. He sounded relieved. 'You are a witch. So you know how to heal him. Lift the curse on my father, and we will let you go.'

Alizon shook her head slowly. 'No. I don't know how to lift this curse. Maybe someone else would, but I don't.'

'Take her home,' John said. His eyes closed – he sounded exhausted. 'If she can't help me, take her back to her hovel.'

Alizon's eyes darted to the wooden dog in Abraham's hand. She gathered all her courage and asked, 'May I take the…?'

Before she could finish, Abraham thrust Night

into his coat pocket and pushed her back through the door.

'Please?' Alizon tried again.

'No.'

The way home in the cart was a lot faster. Alizon closed her eyes when she stepped inside and she must have slept, because when she opened them again the door was being opened and they were back at the Tower. Abraham stood aside as she got out, then mounted his horse again and left. He didn't say a word, and he didn't look back.

14

Thunder rolling
  Lightning burning
  The storm will come
  Will come for you
  It had been a strange few days.

1612

When she arrived home, shaken and terrified, Elizabeth and Old Demdike were sitting together inside the house, and Jennet was playing outside. Alizon pushed open the door, walked inside and covered her face with her hands.

'What's the matter, girl?' Elizabeth asked.

Alizon sighed deeply and, seeing no other way, told them everything. They listened silently, and when she finished, Elizabeth's eyebrows were raised.

'You were stupid to get yourself in trouble,' was Elizabeth's guarded response.

'I know. I know.' It felt cathartic to have told them, to have emptied herself of the gross secret. 'I'm stupid, I know. I didn't know my power. I didn't know what I could do.'

Old Demdike shook her head while Elizabeth nodded hers.

'I am glad you protected yourself,' Old Demdike said sagely, 'we need you.'

Elizabeth shook her head now. 'But I worry about what will happen to this family, to our reputation. This man sounds like a danger. At least we know you have some skill.' She looked at her daughter with grudging respect.

Alizon still felt like she was recovering. She wondered now whether the incident had taken something out of her, had left her injured, because she still felt foggy and tired. She had left the garden for several days, done no weeding, no planting, and nothing had been said about it. Maybe she had some control, now, though the price didn't seem to be worth it.

Alizon's mind kept creeping back to the disabled man in his bed. Whenever she thought of it, she cringed with embarrassment, horror. She knew it was a sin (another sin), but she just couldn't accept that she had done it. That it had been her fault. But, of course, it had.

Three days after Abraham had taken her, she woke up late. Elizabeth and Jennet had already got up, and she hadn't heard them. It was unusual, but she had been so tired.

She raised herself up to sitting, stretched and yawned. It felt cold today, cooler than it had been for several days. She wondered whether snow would come. It was unusual, but snow sometimes came at this time.

Alizon wrapped her shawl around her. She made her way through to the other room, thinking of breakfast. She was pleased to see that Elizabeth or Jennet had made the fire, and it was crackling away. Alizon took a hunk of bread and sat on the stool next to Old Demdike's chair. She was fast asleep, her eyelids flickering. Alizon leaned forward to warm her hands on the fire.

After a few minutes, Old Demdike's eyes began to open. They were both milky white, and Alizon knew that the only thing she would be able to see in this room was, vaguely, the dancing flames.

'Good morning, Grandmother,' Alizon said, so that she would know she was there.

'Is it? Look at the fire,' her grandmother replied.

Old Demdike often said strange things these days, always to do with the fire, and so Alizon ignored her. If you took everything Old Demdike said as counsel, you would have been killed many times over.

'It is a cold one today. Are you warm enough?' Alizon was keen to change the subject. She leaned forward to poke the fire.

Old Demdike must have spotted the movement. 'Stop!' she cried. 'Did you touch the fire? I've seen something terrible. Today, it will happen. Today. Today.'

Alizon sighed. These warnings and threats had been coming for the last few months. Always, they were imminent, always, they were terrible.

There were flecks of spittle on Old Demdike's chin. She was so old. Her mind was gone. She should be put out of her misery, Alizon thought, before she tried to claw it back. She knew what evil thoughts could do now.

'Look, you fool, look at the fire!' Old Demdike cried. 'They are on their way!'

She began to rock in her chair, back and forward, until Alizon feared that she would fall. She reached forward and grabbed the arms of the chair so that it couldn't rock any more.

'No one's on their way, Grandma. No one's coming,' Alizon said in what she hoped was a calming voice.

'No, not no one! Not no one! Someone! You think I'm a fool, girl?' The eyes were steady now, staring in her direction. The change in Old Demdike unsettled Alizon.

'Of course not, Grandma,' Alizon said soothingly. She tried to move the hand on her arm, but the brittle fingers were gripping tightly. The long, greyish fingernails dug into her skin. She couldn't believe that the old woman had so much strength.

'Mark my words. Maybe I'll go first, but you'll go second.'

Alizon shuddered. Strange old woman. She stroked the hand clinging on to her arm and pasted a smile onto her face. She was sure Old Demdike would be able to sense a smile.

'Thank you for warning me, Grandma. I know that you are so wise. You have so much power to be able to see these things.'

'It's not my power. You know whose power it is.' Old Demdike loosened her grip and Alizon took the opportunity to rub her arm where those fingernails had clawed at her.

'Whatever happens, I'll take care of you.' It was Alizon's turn to place a hand on her grandmother's arm, but she did it gently. She suddenly felt very protective.

'You can try,' was all Old Demdike said. She closed her eyes, as if she had begun to dream again.

Alizon thought about walking into the forest, maybe checking her rabbit traps, but no, she couldn't rouse herself to go. She decided to do some mending; there was a pile of rags in the corner that could be sewn into passable dresses or cloaks. She settled on the stool, and began to sew.

It was difficult, though; her fingers were cold and her stitches kept going wrong. She got frustrated, and instead ripped the fabric apart. It had felt satisfying, but now there was even more work to do.

She stood up, walked around the room again, stopped. What was that noise? She listened closely, heard nothing but the snores of her grandmother. But then – there it was again! Alizon walked to the door, opened it a little and peered out. And suddenly, round the side of the hill, she saw a horse, a man, coming this way. She slammed the door and stepped back. No good came from men on horseback.

Old Demdike still slept. What was the man doing here? He must be coming to the Tower. There was no other reason anyone would come down here, it wasn't a through road.

Alizon gathered her courage, strode to the door, opened it wide and gasped. Standing in front of her was an official wearing a uniform of dark green. He carried a sword around his waist.

'Alizon Device?'

Alizon nodded.

The man was holding a scroll. He unrolled it and read. 'Alizon Device. You are summoned to appear before Roger Nowell at Read Hall on this day, 30 March 1612.' He stopped reading from the paper, looked up and said, 'I am to escort you there now.'

Alizon had never heard of Roger Nowell. She glanced around at Old Demdike; her eyes were open, staring blankly in their direction.

'Why?' Alizon asked. She couldn't see a way out of this – if the man wanted her to go with him, she would have to go with him. The sword told her that.

'Mr Nowell will explain all when we arrive. Come.'

The man stood aside and Alizon walked past him and out of the house. She saw no reason to say anything to Old Demdike, she would have heard everything.

The man led her to his horse. In one swift move, he lifted her onto the horse and then climbed on in front of her. The first time she had been on a horse. This was a week of firsts.

The horse wheeled around and Alizon almost fell off, before she managed to grab part of the saddle. Uncomfortably, she clung on as the horse trotted. It was a close call, but she thought she preferred that dark, jolting cart to this. She was too high up, the ground too far away.

As they travelled, Alizon tried to engage the man in conversation, but he ignored her. It could be that someone wanted to use her services – that was a reasonable option. Perhaps word had got out about how she dealt with John Law and now this Roger Nowell wanted her to do something similar. Yes. She wondered how she would respond. She didn't like what she had done to John, but maybe, if she was offered enough money, she would be able to do it again. She would need Night back, of course.

They had skirted around the village and now they were on an open road, well travelled and busy. They often came across other people, either walking or on horseback too, but the man did not talk to any of them, though they tipped their hats at him.

Gradually, buildings appeared on the sides of the road; they were approaching a town. Bigger by far than any place Alizon had been before.

'Where are we?' Alizon asked, expecting no reply.

'Clitheroe.'

'Are we nearly at Read Hall?'

'No.'

Alizon had heard of Clitheroe, the nearest big town. She had never had the need to visit, but people often went there for the market, and it looked like it was a market day today. It was so busy, throngs of people everywhere. The horse took them through what appeared to be the very centre of the town. There was the stench of waste, the road was filthy. There was shouting and crying, a mesh of animal and human sounds barraging Alizon's ears. Stalls were set up along the road, and the houses clustered overhead.

Alizon saw fruit and vegetables for sale, meat, pots and pans, chickens, all sorts. The sellers were shouting their prices, people were arguing and haggling. There was a fight. She had never seen so many people in one place. She tried to take it all in, but by the time the houses began to thin out again she felt exhausted. Too many people, coughing and hacking and yelling. How did they live there, all together like that?

So many firsts.

As they continued, the sky darkened. It had been bright, but now there were clouds overhead. Yellow clouds. The wind whipped up too; it was an evil, icy wind full of knives. Alizon wished she had more clothes. She was numb with the cold. The skies opened, hailstones flew down upon them, thrown into their faces by the wind. They pinched Alizon's skin, and battered her.

'Should we find shelter?' she called.

'Not yet,' the man replied.

Alizon could not ever remember being so cold. At least if she had been walking, her body would have been working, warming itself from the inside. She tried to wrap an arm around herself, but she became too unsteady on the horse, so she had to keep her hands on the saddle. They became numb, didn't feel like hers any more. They were blotchy and purple; they felt raw.

Eventually, they reached a huge wall with a giant wrought-iron gate which stood open. The wall stretched as far as Alizon could see. Through the gate, the road was well kept and even. No holes, no puddles, just an expanse of trampled ground. To either side of the road, there were grass fields with lines of trees. Again, it was beautifully kept. Alizon saw a lake, its surface broken by the incessant hail.

They turned a corner and Alizon gasped. The hugest building she had ever seen. It was taller than the treetops, wider than the river. There were blank glass windows staring down at her: countless windows. It was made of reddish brick. Alizon was used to buildings made of timber, like her home and most of those in the village, or stone, like the church. The bricks distorted her view; she found it difficult to determine the shape of the building because it was so big.

They reached a front door. It was twice the height of Alizon, and wider than her outstretched arms. It was made of a dark, shining wood and in the very centre, bigger than Alizon's head, was a lion head knocker, growling at her.

The man dismounted and helped Alizon

down. Another man in a matching uniform appeared and led the horse away. The man pushed the door open and led Alizon inside.

A cavernous hallway, echoing and empty. The floor was made of intricately patterned tiles, the walls more varnished wood.

Although Alizon wanted to take everything in, the man did not let her linger and instead led her through a door to her right. It was another large room, with tall windows and tapestries on the walls. There was an enormous chair – everything here was so big, giants could have lived there – behind a carved, wooden table. Against the wall with the windows, there was a long, low bench. The man gestured that Alizon should sit there, and then left, closing the door behind him.

It was warmer in here. Alizon noticed that there was a fire lit in the fireplace behind the giant's chair. She rubbed her hands together, thought about whether she was brave enough to move closer. Before she could decide, the door opened again. A different man in the same uniform gestured someone through the door, and closed it again.

Alizon peered at the person she now shared the

room with. He turned around, and both of them strode towards each other, embraced. James. Her brother.

'What are you doing here?' they both said.

Alizon explained the man, and the horse. James nodded. It had been a long time since she had seen James, and she was distraught to see that he looked ill, and drawn with dark shadows under his eyes.

'The same thing happened to me. Barged into my lodgings. I was about to go and find some work when there was this banging on my door. Man with a scroll. He just brought me here, no talking or anything.'

James shivered and Alizon led him closer to the fire.

'But what are we doing here? Who is this Roger Nowell?' Alizon's theory seemed completely wrong, now that her brother was here. What did he have to do with anything?

'You— you don't know who he is?'

James looked pale. Alizon shook her head, but before James could answer, the door opened again and they both wheeled around.

Someone else was thrust into the room, wearing a dark cloak over their head. Slowly they lowered the cloak, and there – standing in the middle of the room, jaw clenched – was Elizabeth. Their mother. Her eyes raked slowly around the room before settling on them.

'Ah,' Elizabeth said slowly. 'A family reunion.' She walked up to James, peered into his face. 'You're getting old.'

James didn't have time to react. Another door near the fireplace was opening now.

A man walked into the room. He was richly dressed, in velvet and silk, a huge cloak enveloping him. He was not a giant. In fact, as he sat in the enormous throne, it became clear that he was actually very small.

He had a pointed, brown beard and beady black eyes which peered at all of them.

'Take a seat.' His voice was strangely high-pitched.

The three of them walked over to the bench and sat. As it was facing the door rather than the table, Alizon had to lean around her brother and mother to see. What was going on?

'I am Sheriff Roger Nowell,' he said. 'You are here because I am investigating claims of witchcraft in this area. I have heard from witnesses who have given me your names. You are Elizabeth, Alizon and James Device, correct?'

Alizon was too shocked to answer, but James and Elizabeth nodded. She felt very cold again, cold to her bones.

'Elizabeth Device, stand.' Roger leaned forward over the table when Elizabeth moved to the centre of the room, taking in her lopsided eyes and apparently leering mouth.

'Elizabeth Device, what do you know of witchcraft in this area?'

'Nothing.'

'Have you ever carried out witchcraft?'

'No.'

'Do you know anyone who has carried out witchcraft?'

'No.'

'Have you ever promised a spell in return for riches?'

'No.'

'Is it true that your mother has a mark of the Devil upon her?'

Silence.

'An answer is required. Is it true that your mother has a mark of the Devil upon her?'

'Yes.' The answer was small.

Alizon felt her eyes widen in shock. A mark of the Devil? Why would she tell the man this?

Roger Nowell smiled grimly and dipped a quill in ink. There was silence for a few moments, apart from the scraping of his quill on parchment, and then he said, 'Very well, Mother Device. You may sit.'

Elizabeth returned to the bench and avoided Alizon's eyes. She looked stonily forward, her chin resting on her clasped hands.

'James Device, stand.'

James gulped, stood.

'James Device, what do you know of witch-craft in this area?'

James seemed to be considering his answer. He kept looking at Alizon and Elizabeth, then back at Roger.

'I only know— I've only heard of— I don't know,' James stuttered.

'What have you heard?'

'I don't know.'

'James Device. There are serious accusations and if you are found to be lying to me, you will be convicted and suffer pain of death. James Device. Have you ever heard accusations against your sister, Alizon Device?'

James raised his eyes to Alizon's. He looked like a frightened animal. 'Yes.'

'And what accusations are these?'

'I…' He was mumbling, Alizon could barely hear him. 'I heard about a young girl, a few months ago, it was claimed that she cursed her.'

'And do you believe these accusations?'

'I don't know.'

Alizon couldn't breathe. Why would James lie? Did he still hate her so much, after what she had accused him of?

More scraping of the quill. 'You may sit.'

James sat, and avoided Alizon's eyes. There was a pause now. Alizon felt strangely calm. She was, however, confused about this girl James had mentioned. What girl? Why did he say it? Roger was looking over another piece of parchment. Raising his eyebrows occasionally. He put it aside.

'Alizon Device, stand.'

Alizon stood, her legs jelly. Roger Nowell's expression was severe.

'Alizon Device, I assume you know why you are here?'

Alizon nodded.

'Then explain.'

'I'm here because of John Law. My familiar – I didn't realise it was my familiar – but I got angry when John called me a thief and I was so cross I just... my familiar... I cursed him, disabled him. I thought he would die. I was so angry. The Devil must have showed me how.'

Silence. Roger looked at her closely. 'So you admit it?' he said quietly.

Alizon nodded.

'What else do you know about witchcraft in the area, Alizon?' His voice was excited now.

'I... I don't know...' She turned to look at James and her mother. Those unexplained thoughts about Jennet, her mother's work, her grandmother... but she couldn't do it. She wouldn't say it.

'Tell me about Anne Whittle,' Roger said. He was standing now.

'Anne...?'

'Anne Whittle! Old Annie! You know her!'

Old Annie. More thoughts and confused memories were flooding back to her, the abbot's skull that had somehow disappeared from their home.

'Yes. I've heard rumours about Old Annie. She

and her daughter stole from us once, I think they stole... and she might have killed my father, John Device! And there was another man who died too.' Her voice broke. 'John Robinson.'

Roger was scratching with his quill. Alizon felt peace inside. She had admitted her sin in hurting John Law. Maybe, now, she would be forgiven. And John – her John – she wanted desperately to know what had happened to him. She wasn't sure why she had mentioned his name in relation to Old Annie and not her own family. It had come out suddenly, an incomplete thought.

Roger stopped writing and rubbed his hands together. 'Very well,' he said briskly. 'Elizabeth Device and James Device, you may leave. I can't spare horses. You will have to walk back to Pendle.'

Elizabeth and James left the room, neither of them looking at Alizon.

'Alizon Device. I am imprisoning you on suspicion of witchcraft. You will stay here while I finish my investigation.'

There was feverish excitement on his face and it terrified Alizon. Perhaps she would not be given her forgiveness after all.

A man appeared silently at her side, grabbed

her arm and pulled her away as she tried to shake him off. Through the grand hallway and another door, down a dark, shadowy staircase, sliding on damp, stone steps, through another door, banging shut behind her, bolts sliding.

She was alone. The room was completely dark, so she felt her way around it, trying to get some idea of her surroundings. It was a small, low-ceilinged room: stone walls, mud floor. There was moisture streaming down the walls and pooling on the floor. It was cold in here, far colder than it had been upstairs, and she huddled herself into a corner.

She still felt surprise at seeing her brother and mother. She supposed that Abraham had told the sheriff about her, but then why had James and Elizabeth been part of this? There was concern in her stomach. She felt as though so much was hidden from her. But, she considered, her information about Old Annie was surely valuable. And, when she thought about her father and John Robinson, it seemed likely that Old Annie had had something to do with it, and surely murder was worse than accidentally disabling a man. She would probably be freed when Roger questioned Old Annie. Yes. She would probably get a reward for her information, and forgiveness for her little mistake. Yes.

With these comforting thoughts in her mind, Alizon fell asleep.

15

The power takes you
   Crushes you
   Sabotages you
   Makes you

1612

Alizon began to hum a tune. She wasn't sure how long she had been there for; in the dark, it was so difficult to measure the passing of time. She had slept twice – but she didn't know how long for – and she had woken up hungry. No one had brought her food and very little to drink, so she had licked moisture from the walls – it tasted fairly clean.

In a rush, the words to the tune came back to her.

'Take a key key and lock padlock her up,

Lock padlock her up, lock padlock her up,
Take a key key and lock padlock her up,
My fair lady.'

The song Jennet had sung once upon a time. Alizon laughed. The irony was too much for her. Her laugh became a howl and there was a banging on the door.

'Stop that!' a voice shouted. 'You won't be down here much longer.'

Muffled voices, boots on stairs, fading away.

It sounded like she would be freed. Perhaps Old Annie had admitted to her crimes too. So she could head home soon. When she got home, Alizon decided, things would change. The Devil had chosen her, for whatever reason, her family too, and she had begun to accept that. But from now on, she would be looked after. She could have admitted all manner of things about her family, but she hadn't. And for that, she should be thanked. No more menial labour – she would never spend hours in that garden again!

No, she had served her penance and life from now on would be more comfortable. It was only what she deserved.

'Take a key key and lock padlock her up,
Lock padlock her up, lock padlock her up,

Take a key key and lock padlock her up,
My fair lady.'

Footsteps, the bolt, a face underlit by a candle. The face looked scared.

'Alizon Device. You're to come with me.'

Looking closely, Alizon saw that this was just a boy, maybe thirteen or fourteen. He avoided her eyes, looking instead at her muddy, ragged dress and her matted hair.

Alizon stood. She felt unsteady, hadn't walked for a long time. The boy took her arm.

'This way, miss, I mean, mistress, I mean…'

Alizon laughed and the boy stopped talking, looked at her in fear.

'Don't curse me, please, I didn't mean nothing by it, I'm just doing as Sheriff Nowell says.'

Alizon was surprised. 'Oh I wouldn't curse you!' She smiled. 'You've done nothing to me.'

The boy's face relaxed into a relieved smile, just as they reached the top of the stairs.

'Oh, heavens,' a rough voice said, 'she hasn't bewitched you has she, you fool! Didn't I warn you?'

It was another man in the same uniform. How did they tell one another apart? The boy shook his head vigorously and the man took her arm now, led her through to the room with the huge chair.

Nowell was sitting there, palms pressed together, a smile on his face.

'Ah, Alizon,' he said. 'Your information has led to the arrest of Anne Whittle and Anne Redferne. Elizabeth Device's information has led to the arrest of Elizabeth Southern.'

Alizon furrowed her brow. Roger nodded his head towards the back of the room.

Alizon turned and her stomach dropped. They never usually used her actual name. But there was Old Demdike, looking tiny and lost, her blank eyes gazing around the room.

Next to her, Old Annie. Alizon couldn't remember the last time she had seen her, but she looked just like Old Demdike, though her teeth had gone, her lips pulled over her gums. Then there was Anne Redferne. She was standing tall. The look she gave Alizon was one of hatred. Alizon quickly turned back to Roger.

'The four of you will be taken to Lancaster Gaol, to await your trial. May God save your souls.' Another of his smiles.

Gaol? Gaol? This wasn't how it was supposed

to go. Unless… unless they needed her and Old Demdike as witnesses at the others' trials. That could be right. Could be.

More uniformed men in the room ushered them out. A carriage – not a cart, a carriage! – bars on the windows, locks on the door, hard seats, malevolent eyes shining back at her. Movement.

'Grandma? They didn't hurt you?' Alizon found her grandmother's hand, clasped it.

'I told you they were coming, you fool.' Her voice was tired, the cloudy eyes distant.

Alizon leaned back, head against the rocking wood. 'Have you seen what will happen to us?'

'You don't want to know, girl.'

A snorting. Anne Redferne. 'You think Old Demdike can tell the future? That old fraud?'

'Settle.' This was Old Annie. She lisped from a lack of teeth.

Anne looked at her, closed her mouth.

'What of my mother and brother?' Alizon asked.

'Safe and free,' was the response from Old Demdike. 'For now.'

Alizon felt relief. Thank goodness that James at least, innocent as he was, was separated from all of this.

'Where is Lancaster Gaol?' Alizon asked.

It was Old Annie who answered. 'A long way from here. I spent time in Lancaster as a child. Here, there and everywhere I would go. Lancaster is a day's walk from Whalley, that I know. With the horses, it'll be less but they're carrying a load. I'd say six hours if the road is good.' She smiled to herself. Memories of happier times, perhaps.

'Six hours!' Alizon exclaimed. The furthest she had ever travelled. She couldn't imagine what it would be like there, so far away.

'Yes, six hours, so you have plenty of time to get your story straight,' said Anne, her voice all rage.

'My story?' Alizon asked.

'Your story. I know why we're here, I know what you said!' she spat.

Alizon shrugged. She had other people to protect, Old Demdike beside her, her brother, herself… and if that meant Old Annie and Anne getting what they deserved, well, that was that.

'I'll…' Anne leaned forward to grab at Alizon, but her mother laid a conciliatory arm on her.

'No.'

Anne sat back, looked down at Old Annie.

She was smiling away still. 'We'll get our chance,' Old Annie said in a sing-song voice.

They didn't talk again for the rest of the journey. There were many things that Alizon wanted to say to Old Demdike, but she didn't dare when Old Annie and Anne were listening. Instead, Alizon tried to sleep, and she managed a few hours in an uncomfortable hunched position.

The coach driver seemed to be in a hurry; he worked the horses hard and didn't stop to give them a break, so they arrived in Lancaster before it was dark. Even though they were locked in their carriage with no windows, they heard the crowds and knew they were entering the city. The carriage slowed. Alizon imagined it weaving through throngs of people, like the streets they had seen in Clitheroe.

Eventually, the carriage halted. She heard the clomping of boots, keys in locks, then the door was opened. Alizon, being closest to the door, was dragged out first. She blinked in the sunlight. A huge, bear-like man cuffed heavy irons around her wrists, a chain between them. It hurt, and Alizon began to feel very, very worried. She knew what happened to witches. Not only death, but hellfire after that.

Alizon was pushed forward, she looked back to

check on Old Demdike but she couldn't see her; there were people everywhere and she was being shoved. Before her was an imposing stone castle, with two towers at the front – between them a dark, studded door. The door opened, it seemed by itself, and Alizon was led inside and down dark, steep stairs. She was getting used to being led underground.

At the bottom of the stairs was a candle-lit corridor, dank and musty. The echoing drip of water filled the air. Alizon was pushed into what felt like a small, damp cave. The door was covered with strips of metal, and before it was banged shut, Old Demdike was thrown in behind her. The old woman, her hands cuffed, her eyes unseeing, lost her balance and fell forward. Alizon managed to catch her just before she hit the floor. Alizon gently lowered her grandmother to a seated position, before looking at her surroundings.

The stench was the biggest thing. It was foul: blood and sweat and faeces and terror. She knew she would not be licking moisture from the floor in this cell. Apart from the door, there were no other openings, no window, but she could see fairly well because of the candles in the corridor outside; the light meandered in through the bars on the door. The air was thick, wet in her throat. There was a strange, echoing moaning coming from somewhere nearby.

Although this was a terrible, terrible place, Alizon was glad that they had at least been separated from Old Annie and Anne. She could talk freely with Old Demdike now.

'What did they do to you, Grandma?' she asked.

'Came to the Tower two days after they took you,' she wheezed, as though it was difficult for her to talk. 'That Nowell questioned me. Bitch of a daughter told him I had the mark of the Devil. I got angry. Told him of course I did, I sold my bloody soul to the Devil. Didn't ask any more questions. Just took me here.'

Alizon sighed. 'Do you think he will help us out of this?'

Old Demdike's voice became sharp. 'Who?'

'Him. The... the Devil.' Alizon knew the answer by the expression on her grandmother's face.

A snort. 'I won't make it out of here. You will, but not for long. Why would the Devil care to help us?'

'I thought... I thought...' It was hard to put into words. 'Because. Because the pastor always said God helps those in need and I thought... I thought...'

A cackle. 'You thought the Devil is some caring father? Tell me. Look at my life and tell me. When has the Devil helped me? A little extra money. A little extra life. But I'd have been better off dying a long time ago.'

Alizon felt everything slipping away from her. All of her fear of God, of sin, of doing the wrong thing, had been replaced. When she made her decision to give up her hair to her mother, used her familiar and was lost to God, she had thought, had felt, as though she had moved into someone else's caring arms. And yes, she had thought, perhaps, that she was protected. There had been something sitting, curled around her heart. She felt it there. She felt its purpose. But now, with her grandmother's words, she felt it shrivel up and die, leaving her heart weak and exposed.

'So what will happen? she asked, aghast.

'I'm blind, girl. What do you expect me to see?'

'But you always… in the fire?'

'Almost everything I saw has already happened. I can't see anything new here. There is no fire.'

'Almost everything? Then what else have you seen?'

'The darkness.'

More riddles. Would anyone ever just speak

sense to her? She had spent her life stumbling through fog, making wrong decision after wrong decision. Everything hidden from her, meaning and purpose always just out of reach.

'Why did you do all of this?' Alizon asked desperately. 'Would it not have been better to live a humble, God-fearing life?'

Old Demdike was silent for a few moments. She was far away, a life in reverse flying before her. There was no sound but the drip, drip of water and a scurrying of rats.

'I made my choices, girl, and you made yours. There is no turning back. There is no second chance. I had to do what I did. When your mother was born, everything changed. Old Annie... she... she caused this. I feel it. I know it.'

Alizon felt like punching the wall. 'You never speak plainly, do you? Everything has to be shrouded. Everything mysterious. Can't you just answer my question?'

Old Demdike looked affronted. 'You have no right to speak to me like that.'

'I have and I do. I am here because of you.'

'You are here because of you.'

'No. All of my life, I have followed. I have tried

to be guided. I have tried to do the right thing. But that is impossible with you. You and my mother have done all you can to ruin my life. That is clear.'

'You think that? All the choices I made were for the good of my family. I would never harm my flesh and blood. Your mother had a brother, Robert. Another brother, who came to harm because of me. That day... everything became evil. But since then, all my choices have been for the good of all of you.'

Alizon snorted.

'If you have done all of this for the good of me, why didn't you let me marry John?' The question bubbled to the surface before Alizon could stop it.

'Who?'

The response made Alizon feel raw fury. That John Robinson could be snuffed out and forgotten. Who, other than her, remembered him now?

'So, you deny it?'

'Girl. I have no idea who you are talking about.'

Alizon felt the anger course through her, down to her toes, through her fingertips. She raised her hand, fire pumping through her, and slapped her grandmother on the face. Old Demdike's head snapped back and slammed into the wall. Being unable to see, she hadn't been able to prepare for the violence, and now she slid down to the floor, unconscious.

As soon as it happened, Alizon wished she could take it back. She lifted her grandmother, shook her, but she wouldn't wake up. She was still breathing, and that was a relief, but her eyes wouldn't open. Alizon laid her carefully on the floor, among the mud and filth, and crouched in the opposite corner, head in hands. Everything was wrong. Everything was so wrong.

16

Convulsion, paroxysm,
  Laceration, malady,
  The pain will grow,
  Will grow

1612

It was a long time before Old Demdike opened her eyes. A hunk of bread had been thrown into the cell while Old Demdike was still asleep, which Alizon ate ravenously (she had thought of saving some for her grandmother, but it was gone before she knew it and barely quelled the pain in her stomach), and it seemed a very long time since that had happened. Maybe some hours, maybe some days, it was impossible to tell.

But now she was stirring. Her blank eyes opened, a grimace of pain on her face.

'Where… am I?' she muttered, bony fingers scraping the ground.

'With me,' Alizon replied. She saw the memories flood back to Old Demdike, the reality of her situation etched on her face.

A scowl, another grimace. A hand went to the back of her head, but she couldn't see the coagulating blood on her fingers. Alizon shuddered. She wanted to apologise for hitting her, but the guilt stilled her tongue.

'Water?' Old Demdike croaked.

'None.' It was the necessary reply.

Old Demdike closed her eyes again, frowns and flickers fluttering over her face.

'The darkness is closer,' she murmured, her face grey.

'What is the darkness?' Alizon tried again. She was desperate for answers, her mind stretching and tensing, trying to fill gaps and lighten dark corners.

'I see my darkness. I don't see yours. There is no need for you to worry,' Old Demdike sighed, the words escaping her like she was deflating.

'You… I will be freed?' Alizon asked, a small bubble of hope filling her chest. There was no answer.

Alizon nursed the little bubble through the silence which rolled out ahead of them, like smoke.

Alizon closed her eyes. The hope sat there, but her head was pounding; she was too thirsty, her mouth dry. She could hear the dripping moisture somewhere and it made her thirstier still, but she couldn't bear to lick these filthy walls. If what Old Demdike had said was true, though, then hopefully she would soon be free.

And then, the guilt falling on her like a stone, she realised what Old Demdike had said. She had seen her own darkness. Alizon had ignored it, focusing on her light, but it sounded like…

Alizon looked over at her grandmother. Her eyes were closed, her face grey. She looked so small, a pile of bones under a cloak. There was no movement.

Alizon put her ear to her grandmother's mouth. She shook her. She lifted her, tried to heave her up. She dropped her, and her head cracked against floor. Nothing. Her grandmother was dead.

A wail escaped her. It was loud, animal. She felt so alone. More alone than she had ever been. Her grandmother looked as though she had been turned to stone. Alizon was lost, with just this statue. The darkness had come for her grandmother.

Another wail. And another.

Her grandmother had always been there. All her life, she had always been there. But now she had left her, at the time when she most needed someone. She was all alone.

And then, another wave of guilt. She had hit Old Demdike. She had killed her. First, she had hurt John Law, now she had killed her own grandmother. She had felt that electricity coursing through her again, just the same as when she had hurt him. She knew, now, that that was the Devil working through her. The Devil had taken her, and was using her as a plaything.

There – in the dark corner of the cell – she saw it. A huge, black dog with glowing eyes. Night. Staring at her. Her familiar, here again.

She hugged her legs with her arms, hid her face so that she couldn't see the dog, and moaned and wailed.

A clanking sound. Marching feet. Metal on metal. The door was open.

'Stop that sound.' A gruff voice. 'You'll be heard in the centre of the city.'

Alizon raised her arm and pointed at the monstrous dog sitting in the corner. The guard looked, saw nothing, shrugged and turned to leave. But then he stopped. He had noticed the statue.

A shout. More marching feet, faster this time. A body bundled out of the cell. Metal on metal again, and Alizon was completely alone: even Night had gone.

The wailing had stopped. Alizon had run out of sound. There was nothing left inside her. The bubble inside her had escaped; she was empty. She knew that even if she was released – and she found that very unlikely now that she had killed her grandmother – she would be haunted for the rest of her days by the knowledge of what she had done. There was a darkness inside her now. It had left Old Demdike and made its way into her.

What was going to happen now? What was going to happen to her?

Alizon knew that she was a selfish person. She had always wanted the best for herself, without thinking of others, and look where it had left her. She thought now of her mother, that woman she had come to dislike and who had surely disliked her back. She thought of her sister, that strange child she had avoided where possible and shown no love to. She thought of her brother, clutching and grabbing and robbing.

The lot of them were selfish. A plague. The work her mother had done, and her grandmother too, and her in the end – it hadn't helped. They hadn't done good things. She deserved to be here.

She now pictured her mother and sister at Malkin Tower. She wondered whether Elizabeth was happy to be rid of her. She wouldn't know that Old Demdike was dead – who would tell her? She thought about them carrying out their daily tasks. Would they miss Alizon's scavenging and gardening and mending, even if they didn't miss her? She felt something she had never felt before. Homesickness. She wished, more than anything else, to be back at Malkin Tower. Her straw bed would seem a luxury compared to the filthy, hard cell. There would be a pot of rabbit stew on the fire (a fire! Imagine a fire!) and a small beer to drink. She would feel content and warm, her belly full and her mind empty. Old Demdike would be sitting in her chair. She might be telling one of her stories; she could still see, she would be her old sharp self.

Elizabeth would walk in; she might even smile at Alizon and thank her for the stew. Jennet, as a happy, young child, would dance around their feet…

She slept. Confusing, angry dreams full of blood and red. Looking down at her hands to see the shining, crimson liquid. Faces flashing through her mind, one after the other, people she had hurt.

Alizon awoke with an aching back and neck from the unusual position she had been hunched in. She stretched as much as she could and gazed blearily around. There was a piece of bread on the floor; it must have been left there as she slept, sitting in a puddle of filth. She snatched it up and wolfed it down, gagging at the awful taste as she did so.

She closed her eyes again, and tried to distance herself from her surroundings.

17

Powerful, we rise
  We take
  We kill
  We cry

1612

The lack of a window made the passing of time impossible to measure. Always there was the dripping water, the scrabbling of the rats, but sometimes there was a clanking banging. There might be screams, a moaning. Sometimes she heard men's laughter – the guards, she supposed.

Bread and sometimes water or a foul beer were left; the cell door opened and closed before she could see her attendant's face. Whether it was days or hours apart, she never knew. It was never enough to sate her hunger and thirst.

When it was hot, the stench was unbearable and she would gag and wretch. When it was cold, she hugged herself but couldn't warm.

And so the days passed.

She shared the cell with nothing other than Old Demdike's ghost, who howled and berated her when she tried to sleep.

She knew that when her life finally ended, she would go to Hell, but how could Hell be worse than this?

One day there was a shuffling to match the marching. Metal on metal. The door was opening. A candle, blinking the light away, a shadow, bodies, a moan and thump. The door was closed, and someone else was in the cell.

'Who is that?' Alizon asked, folded up in a corner, afraid.

'Alizon?' came the rasping response. A voice she knew well. Her mother.

'What are you doing here?' Alizon cried, a confusing mix of emotions inside her.

'Same as you, I would think.'

'I thought they set you free? You and James?'

'Well, it seems that we aren't free any longer, me or James.'

'James is arrested too?'

Elizabeth sighed, as if from the realisation that the questions would not stop until she answered them. 'We thought we needed to do something when the arrests happened. A few weeks ago, on Good Friday, we had a gathering at Malkin Tower to see if there was anything to be done. James stole a sheep – that's why he's locked away – and the rest of us were discussing what had happened. Many turned up when the word got out. Lots of women I've helped over the years. Lots of them were worried, too, that they might have done things to get them arrested.'

Alizon nodded in the darkness. She imagined being there, the community gathering round to help. It seemed like a dream. Elizabeth had spent so long helping people with her skills that she must have gained some friends – or at least allies. All while Alizon had been hiding away from everything and everyone.

'We talked over what had happened. Everyone was keen to help Old Demdike. It's not right for her to be taken, at her age. We didn't come to any decisions. We just said that we would support each other, look out for each other. But that sheriff, that Roger Nowell, he found out about it somehow. We were all brought before him, everyone who had been there, and he's decided it was some meeting of witches just because we had it on Good Friday. And he's locked us all away. And… and…' Elizabeth seemed lost, suddenly. Lost and afraid.

Didn't her mother know that Old Demdike was dead? 'And Jennet?' she asked tentatively.

Alizon saw the silhouette of Elizabeth's body droop. 'He took her. The sheriff. He took her into his care, he said. As though she hadn't been cared for by me! But he'll soon find out, oh he'll soon find out. She won't put up with her mother being locked away. She's strong, that girl, stronger than he knows. She will do what's right.'

'But…' Alizon began hesitantly. 'But what could she do? She's just a child. The sheriff won't listen to her, will he?'

'She can do more than you would guess, girl.'

Alizon didn't answer. She was well used to being told how much better Jennet was than her. She promised herself that she would treat her own children equally. None of them would feel like her. She pushed the thought away, remembered what she knew deep inside – she would never have children.

'Oh, are you insulted? The idea that a girl of nine could be more wily than you?' Elizabeth gave a hacking laugh.

'Roger Nowell is a grown, educated man. I don't think he can be tricked,' Alizon retorted.

'He's tricked himself into thinking of our little gathering as a coven of witches, summoning the Devil to wish him harm. If he can believe that, then he can be tricked by my clever daughter.'

Alizon, who thought that actually Roger Nowell had not been far off in his accusations, kept quiet. Her mother had done many questionable things, so why she was now claiming that it was not the case was difficult for Alizon to understand.

'What happens to us now?' Alizon asked, changing the subject. She hadn't talked in such a long time that she was desperate to keep conversing, even if it was with her prickly mother, and even though her throat rasped with the lack of use.

There was a pause. Eventually, Elizabeth replied, 'that all depends.'

'What does it depend on?'

'We go to trial. We are judged. Evidence will

be heard. We will give our evidence too. And then they will decide whether we are witches.'

'And if they do?'

'If they do, we will be sentenced to death.'

A deep, long sigh was Alizon's response.

'There is something we can do,' said her mother. 'You told the sheriff about Old Annie and Anne Redferne. They made accusations against us too. We just need to make sure that they are the ones to be convicted. The things we can say about them. We can build a case against them. We just need to say the same things. James will follow our lead, Old Demdike too.'

So Elizabeth didn't know her own mother was dead, or who had killed her. When to tell her?

'If we can convince them that they are the ones who have done all of this, then maybe we will be freed.'

Her words mirrored a thought that Alizon had had what seemed a long time ago, back at Nowell's house when she'd talked about the theft of the skull. But what Elizabeth was suggesting was different. It seemed that she was suggesting a lie. She was suggesting a fabrication. That seemed wrong, just to save their own skin.

'I know what I have done, Mother. I will be

judged for it, and I hope they will show me kindness. If you are sure of your innocence, then why do we need this plan?'

In the light from the flickering corridor candles, Alizon saw her mother raise her eyebrows.

'You know nothing of men, Alizon. You know nothing of their cowardice and fear. These men do not care for guilt or innocence. They just want to stamp out their own fear. They want to rid the world of things they don't understand, and these men... these men don't understand women. They don't care that the things we did, we had to do. If we didn't make the cures, those people would die for not affording a doctor. If we didn't attend childbirths, well, only noble children would survive. If we didn't do what we did to solve disputes and help people who have been wronged, or need love, or revenge, society would fall apart. We do what is necessary. And they would kill us for it.'

Alizon stared at her mother. Had she really tricked herself into thinking that witchcraft was for the good? 'Mother... you know what I did. The Devil helped me to gravely injure John Law. Others have done terrible things, too. We are not talking about doing things for good, we are talking about doing things for ill.'

Elizabeth peered through the gloom of their cell at Alizon. 'You believe that to be true?'

'I know it to be true. And...' Now that her mother was talking so freely, an opportunity for more of the truth. 'And John Robinson was murdered. Someone must pay for that sin.'

Was there a glint of recognition in Elizabeth's eyes when that name was spoken? She said nothing.

'John Robinson was murdered and that wasn't for good,' Alizon repeated, trying to incite a response.

'You thought you could get away, didn't you?' Elizabeth said. 'You always thought yourself better than us. You think we didn't see you, looking down your nose at us, thinking us filthy and disgusting? The times you thought us evil? The way you looked at me when I brought Jennet home? This life is filthy and disgusting. You can try and try to claw your way out but you'll always end up wallowing in the dirt. You thought if you ran away with that man, that everything would be clean and happy?'

The words had come out in a rush and left Elizabeth panting a little as she circled her daughter. Alizon just stared back at her mother's dimly lit face.

She couldn't bring herself to ask the final question that could lead to the truth. Her mouth opened, and closed again.

'See, you can't deny it! You thought to escape us. We treated you well. You never went hungry, did you? Not really? But you moped around, looking miserable and dragging your feet. You wonder why I prefer Jennet's company to yours? You are unlikeable. You are selfish. You never wanted to be part of our family. Your horrified looks and your muttering. You are exactly where you deserve to be.'

'Anything I did was because of you! I have been unloved and ignored since well before Jennet came along, and you wonder why I tried to get away? So tell me – tell me the truth – did you do it? Did you kill him?'

Elizabeth laughed, a mirthless laugh. 'You overestimate my power. I know about John Robinson because of what you said when the sheriff summoned us, and through what James told me since. Don't you think it proves my point, though, stupid girl? You imagine I would kill a man because he might marry you? You imagine that we were so needful of your… of your what? Your skills? That we would kill a man to stop him taking you? That I would go to the effort?

You thought you were too good for us and you weren't. That is the end of this story. No murder here. No nothing. Stupid girl.'

Alizon leaned against the wet wall of the cell and realised that she was crying. She was glad her mother couldn't see her tears. Perhaps Elizabeth was right. Perhaps she had thought herself better than the rest of her family. But all she had tried to do, always, was the right thing. And now this was where she was. No closer to the truth, with a mother who despised her.

'Then who would do it? If not you, then who?' she sobbed.

'A thief, a robber, a drunk. How should I know? Why should I care? People die all the time.'

'I did try,' Alizon said quietly.

'What?'

'I did try to be a part of the family. After John died. I did try.' She could name on one hand the people who had shown her affection. John Robinson, her brother James, her father John and – occasionally – her grandmother, Old Demdike. Her own mother was a distant, cold woman. Nothing could change that.

'Let me tell you a tale, Alizon.'

It was strange hearing her mother say her

name. It was unusual. She realised that she had been given that name. Who had given it to her, as a screaming infant? Her mother, or her father? Had it been done with love? Her mind was wandering. Elizabeth came closer and clicked her fingers in front of her face.

'Listen. Listen to me. You think you are the only person in this world whose life hasn't gone the way it should have. But you're wrong. You know I had two brothers?'

Alizon nodded.

'One died so I could live. He was healthy and bright, he had no disfigurement.' Elizabeth gestured towards her own face, her eyes at odd angles. 'Who do you think Old Demdike would have preferred to live? Me? Or him?' She waited for an answer.

'Why are you telling me this?'

'Life is hard, Alizon. That's the point I'm making. You were ignored, I was despised, poor Old Demdike had no mother at all, she was murdered. We scratch and scrape and try and make our way. And none of us are happy. The biggest mistake in life is trying to be happy. You need to be powerful. That's what I've been trying to teach you.'

Alizon turned towards the door where the light from the candles flickered, and let the words sink in. Elizabeth retired to the back of the cell as if she felt she had said enough, and she spoke no more. Alizon just contemplated. She knew she was not clever, she often felt as though understanding was just out of her reach. What was right and what was wrong?

Maybe Elizabeth was right. Maybe she had been searching for happiness, and maybe that wasn't possible for people like her. She had tried to do the right thing, that was true, but when Alizon thought about it... she had tried to do the right thing for her. Had she ever properly cared for her family? Yes, she had done so out of obligation, but she had never done so out of love. When Alizon had started helping her family, she had done so because she thought it was the best for her. Perhaps, happiness was reserved for the rich and powerful. People like Roger Nowell, with the halls and servants, they were probably happy. Maybe even the servants, with their wages and their sense of purpose, maybe they were happy. But people who lived in hovels and had a matriarch at the head of their family and no money and no jewels? How could they ever be happy?

Alizon slipped into sleep. She had memories of the door opening, bread being thrown in.

Marching feet. Clanking. Metal on metal.

'Elizabeth Device!' A rough, angry voice.

Her mother was dragged from the cell, kicking and screaming while Alizon cowered against the cell wall. All alone again.

After her mother's shouts died away, Alizon questioned if Elizabeth had ever been there. Or was it her imagination? Had it been Old Demdike's ghost, mocking her? The cell was definitely empty now. No one here but Alizon and her thoughts. The sounds of the cells carried on. Dripping, moaning. There was a scream. There was a bang. When had she last slept? Had it been days ago? Or minutes? A spider crawled towards her. It had sixteen legs and the face of the Devil; it was the size of her palm.

There was a clink, clink, clink noise and then it was gone. But how long had it been gone for? Had it ever existed?

Then marching feet again. Shuffling, dragging. More metal on metal. A body, thrown in a heap into her cell. The door was closed.

A groaning, whimpering sound from the body in her cell. Alizon crawled over to the heap and moved the rags away from the face. It was her mother. Elizabeth had been here after all. She flinched away from her daughter's touch. Who knew how long she had been gone for, where she had been, why she was back now.

Alizon stared at the face. Its eyes were tightly closed, winged and angry. The jaw tight, too. Clenched and solid. Something had happened.

'Did Roger Nowell call for you?' Alizon asked gently.

The eyes opened. Shallow, quick breaths in a sallow face. Sounds, a few sounds, but Alizon couldn't decipher them.

'He did?' she asked again, prompting.

'No,' came the harsh, one-word response.

Elizabeth raised her hands. Alizon was confused, before she realised that Elizabeth was trying to show her them. Alizon took them, and peered closely. Even in the grim half-light of the cell, she could see that there was something wrong. The fingers were dark, bruised beyond recognition. And their shape… some were bent, some shorter than they should be, some longer. The space where the fingernails should have been was a bloody mess.

'What did they do to you?' Alizon whispered. She shifted into a position where she was cradling her mother's head. It felt unusual, being in close contact, but her mother was like a wounded squirrel, broken and sore. She needed comfort.

Elizabeth lay still for a long time. Perhaps she couldn't move. 'They wanted me to confess,' was her eventual, weak reply.

'To confess to what?'

A sigh. A look of derision. It was her mother after all.

'To witchcraft.'

The words were a long way apart. As though wherever they came from, deep down inside, was broken.

'Did you?' Alizon asked. Pure curiosity. She knew her mother was guilty of it, really.

'No. Never.' The eyes closed for some time.

Then they flashed open, an uneven white in the darkness.

'I was told interesting things.' Her voice was stronger.

Alizon didn't reply. She stayed where she was, cradling her head, arms at her sides.

'I was told things I didn't know. I was enlightened. I was told about someone close to us.' Elizabeth seemed to be getting stronger each time she spoke, and all at once she was sitting away from her daughter, using the opposite wall to prop herself up. 'You, Alizon, have something to tell me.'

Now Elizabeth was standing above her in the dim light of the cell.

'What did you do to Old Demdike?'

'What?'

'They told me what happened to Old Demdike. She was here, in this cell.'

'Yes.' This, Alizon could agree with.

'Old Demdike died in this cell.'

'Yes.' Alizon remembered the cold flesh of that dead body.

'She came in with you, alive, and left dead and bloody.'

'Yes.'

'That man, John Law, he crossed you and was left lame and in pain.'

'Yes.'

'John Robinson. He probably crossed you, I think. He was left dead.'

'No!'

'My husband. Your father. Who knows what he did to annoy you. But he died too.'

'What did you say to them?' Alizon stood up. She was horrified, the truth of her mother's words pressing down on her. Had she accused her to their captors? Would she be the one to take the blame for all of this?

Elizabeth turned away from her daughter, and sighed. 'Nothing,' she said. And just like that, Alizon's fear retreated. She felt, in that one word, a support she had been keening for. She felt an ally, someone to stand next to her. Maybe she wasn't alone after all.

'I've done terrible things, Mother. I am guilty, you know this. But not of everything. No, not of everything.'

'The only thing you're guilty of, Alizon, is a lack of brains. We are in here together. If we want to get out, we are going to need to get out together. If we are fighting among ourselves…'

'But you know I have done some terrible things, and I need to atone for them.'

Her mother gave a huge sigh before she spoke again. 'Alizon. I will not die in this place, but if we are going to leave, we are going to leave together. You need to start forgetting the truth. You need to start considering what is for the best. Answer me this question. You say you have done some terrible things. You say you need to atone for them. Are you willing to die for them?'

'If that is what God—'

'God won't be deciding this, those cowardly men will. Are you willing to die for them?'

'If the Devil works through me, then surely God can—'

'The Devil! God! Just answer the question. Are you willing to die for what you have done?'

Alizon was silent. She couldn't picture her own death. She tried to imagine the executioner, the noose, but all she could see was blackness. She wondered whether she would walk out with her head held high, or have to be carried, screaming and thrashing. She thought of the things she had done that filled her with shame. Burning guilt. Could she spend the rest of her life like that? She was disgusted with herself. But, she still couldn't picture her own death. The need to live was too strong. She didn't believe that those men would send her to the grave. No. She couldn't picture it.

'No,' she said quietly.

'Then we need to work together. It was clear what they were doing, those questioners, those torturers. They were trying to split us apart, make us fight against one another and blame one another. If just one of us from Malkin Tower is found guilty, how could they find the others innocent? Would they really believe that the rest of us were ignorant to it?'

Alizon shook her head weakly. She knew herself how hard it had been to keep herself innocent.

Her mother was standing very close to her now. 'So. We need to work together. We need to work together against Old Annie. They want somebody. They are thirsty for blood. So we have to give them somebody. We will work against her and her family.'

'But... but I confessed...'

'Say you were bewitched! You must say you were bewitched by Old Annie. She did it all. Can you say that?'

'I don't know...'

'Can you say that?'

'I don't know...'

The conversation was becoming cyclical. It rose up again after sleep, after food, after time spent comatose on the floor of the cell. Alizon kept expecting the torturers to come for her, but they never did. She realised eventually that because she had already confessed, perhaps they didn't need to. It was still unsettling, the endless waiting for pain that may never come.

Alizon began to get used to the cold, and as soon as she did the season began to change. One day it became unbearably hot. Sticky, stinking, foul. They groaned and moaned, and all around them in other cells they could hear other groans and moans.

Alizon noticed that her bones were showing through her skin, her ribs, her back. Her flesh was disappearing. Perhaps she was disappearing. She could still feel pain. Sores on her legs, around her mouth. Her pain was mirrored in her mother's face.

The conversation had stopped some time ago. They had no energy for talk any more. They just lay on the cold floor that doubled as their bed. But it had been practised and rehearsed, the conversation, so it worked its way around Alizon's head anyway, constant, always there.

After what felt like centuries had passed, there was a shout and shuffling noises outside the cell. Alizon opened her eyes, slowly. There… on the floor… she heaved herself up, as quickly as she could. Food. Hot food. Stew. She shovelled it into her mouth with her bare hand, kicking her mother awake as she did so. Elizabeth made her way over too, and the two of them finished the stew, glorying in the taste of meat. There was beer too, and they both drank heavily. When it was gone, their stomachs hurting from the sudden food, Elizabeth spoke.

'It will happen soon.'

Alizon had no energy to reply, her mind was focused inward, where the stew was digesting. But she knew what her mother meant. The trial was imminent.

18

Like an army
  Like a battalion
  Invading
  Invading
  We will come

18 AUGUST 1612

Clanging and shouting and marching and banging.
The noise was urgent and excited. It was happening.

Metal on metal: the door opened. Light:
torches. Men. Arms pulled forward, put into chains.
A mother and daughter marched, tripping and falling
on unused legs, through a corridor and up steps. Sunlight, painful sunlight, searing into skulls. Then, without warning, a bucket of ice-cold water thrown at
each of them.

Shivering and sweating, led inside. Relief from the sunlight.

A big room. The biggest room. Room full of people, all turning to look. More women, men too, in chains. Old Annie. James. They were all there. A bench at the side of the room, pushed roughly down, chains locked to the floor.

Alizon took a deep breath, trying to bring herself to the room, to get over the shock of leaving the cell. She looked around carefully, trying to take in every little detail. It was like a huge version of the room in Roger Nowell's hall, where he had heard their evidence. The bench that they were sitting on was on the right-hand side. At the back of the hall was a gigantic table topped with quills and scrolls. In front of the table was a wooden block with a large iron ring clamped to it.

And after that, row upon row of wooden benches facing the table and the block. And all of these benches were filled with people, people pointing and whispering and shouting at them, people murmuring and laughing, people making the sign of protection from the evil eye.

Alizon felt herself shrink under their curious gaze. She had never been in front of this many people before, and here they all were, leaning around each other, standing and peering, pulling themselves up on others' shoulders to get a closer look.

A door behind the table opened. A man, wearing a smart blue velvet coat over a ruffled white shirt, came in. He had a large, rotund stomach and a ruddy, pock-marked face. His thinning white hair was brushed back, and his moustache was pointed. He sat in the chair at the centre of the table.

Next, a slightly younger man, wearing black leather and with his long, dark hair slicked back. He sat to the left of the other man.

Behind him, Roger Nowell, his face expanded with self-importance. He sat on the right.

When the three men had sat down, the audience took their seats too, and quieted to a deathly hush.

The man in the middle began to speak.

'I am Sir James Altham. I am joined by Sir Edward Bromley and the prosecutor, Sheriff Roger Nowell. We are here on the grave matter of witchcraft in the region of Pendle in this county of Lancashire. The accused' – he gestured towards the bench, to more muttering from the audience – 'are here because of evidence that they have practised witchcraft for ill, for evil, and even for murder.'

At this last word, the audience began to talk loudly and angrily, and some of the people closest to their bench spat at them.

Sir James seized a wooden hammer and knocked the table in front of him. The audience fell silent again.

'We have many accused here today, and we must proceed as quickly as possible. Therefore, I beg you to be silent while these hearings are in session. Any persons disturbing the swift and necessary course of justice will be removed from this court.'

The crowd looked frightened. Not even the sound of breathing now.

'Anne Whittle will be the first. Ginter, bring Anne Whittle to the stand.'

A rough-looking man with a large burn over the left side of his face grabbed Old Annie. She looked grey, at death's door. Her blind eyes swivelled round and round in her skull. She stumbled as she was dragged, and had to be carried. Ginter threaded her chains through the iron ring in the stand, and left her there in a propped-up position.

'Anne Whittle, you stand accused of the evil murder of Robert Nutter by witchcraft. How do you plead?' Sir James's face was one of disgust at the bag of bones in front of him.

'Not guilty.'

Roger Nowell looked angry now.

Alizon sifted through her memories for Robert Nutter. The Nutters were the farming family, fairly wealthy. Alizon couldn't remember a Robert Nutter. She was confused too; this wasn't what she had accused Old Annie of.

Sir James sighed. 'Anne Whittle. We have evidence against you and a confession from you already. You are guilty.'

'I plead not guilty,' the old woman replied, with more strength than she appeared to have.

'James Robinson. To the stand, please.'

A man pushed his way through the crowd at this order from Sir James. He was about forty years old, his face sunburnt and creased.

'James Robinson. What do you know of Anne Whittle?'

'I knew her twenty years ago.'

Twenty years ago! No wonder Alizon couldn't remember this Robert Nutter.

'She practised witchcraft, I saw it, and people came to her often for her work. Robert Nutter accused her of turning his beer sour. She got angry. She cursed him.'

James nodded at Sir James, who nodded back and dismissed him. James walked back to the crowd.

'That seems damning. Thomas Potts, can you come forward to read Anne Whittle's confession to Roger Nowell?'

A wiry, young man stood. He had been sitting at the side of the table; Alizon hadn't noticed him before. He was eager-looking, and wore an eyeglass. He selected a scroll from the table, unrolled it and began to read.

'On this day Anne Whittle appeared before me and claimed that she had given her soul to a Thing like a Christian man, on his promise that she would not lack anything and would be given any revenge she desired.'

A gasp made its way around the gathered crowd.

Old Annie's face was getting paler and paler. Alizon could imagine her saying those things to Roger Nowell to scare him, to trick him, but now it had been used against her.

'Anne Whittle. The evidence against you is

clear. What say you?' Sir James's hungry face leaned forward.

Old Annie took a few moments to reply. She looked small and terrified, like a caught rabbit. 'Guilty. Guilty. I pray God for forgiveness. It was just me, just me, be merciful to my daughter, it was just me, just me—'

Sir James did not let Old Annie finish. He waved his arm and Ginter carried her away, out of the room. The crowd booed her as she passed.

Through the horror, Alizon felt relief. Old Annie was already damned. Anything else said against her could hardly harm her further. Maybe she and her mother could carry out their plan. Maybe they could do it. Alizon leaned around to peer at Elizabeth, trying to catch her eye, to let her know. But her mother was staring resolutely forward, and did not even flinch when Sir James called, 'Elizabeth Device.'

Alizon watched as though from afar as her mother, her cellmate, was led to the stand. She held herself tall and stared down the judges. They stared back. The clerk, Thomas Potts, looked up and then began writing feverishly, ink splattering as he filled a scroll with spidery writing.

'Elizabeth Device. You are accused of the murders of James Robinson, of Bottle Lane' – this James Robinson Alizon had never heard of, and she wondered how long he had been dead – 'John Robinson' – a sickening, horror-filled moment – 'and Henry Mitton. How do you plead?'

Elizabeth snorted. 'Not guilty. I am not guilty. None of us are guilty. Not of these made-up charges. Those men may have died, but it certainly was not my doing. Your fear is disgusting to me.'

Elizabeth had said this loudly, and was met with yells from the crowd. Sir James and Sir Edward had to stand to hush the audience, banging the hammer and shouting.

When silence finally fell, Sir Edward spoke. His voice was smooth, rich and self-assured. 'There is no fear, here, Elizabeth Device. We are simply looking for the truth. What do you say?'

'I say you are not looking for the truth. You have us here under false pretences. You are the liars. I am innocent. We are all innocent in my family. If you were to convict me, you would be murderers yourselves!' she shouted.

Sir James and Sir Edward were taken aback. There was a pause while they looked at scrolls, and whispered together in hushed tones. Roger Nowell leaned over and began whispering too. The others listened, nodded, came to an agreement.

Sir James spoke. 'We bring to the stand a witness against the accused. Jennet Device.'

Alizon looked at her mother. She didn't seem concerned. But why was Roger Nowell grinning like that?

Jennet was brought to the front of the courtroom. She was wearing a dark green dress –new, she hadn't had that before – and her dark hair was brushed and neat. She looked at her mother, and her eyes were unreadable.

'Jennet Device. Tell me about your mother,' Sir James said encouragingly, in a kindly voice to the nine-year-old girl. Elizabeth smiled at her daughter. She looked confident.

Jennet looked dully at the audience. 'I have reason to believe my mother is a witch…' She paused.

A moment later her words were drowned out. Elizabeth's face had become a mask of fury. She began to scream at her child.

'You foul little hag! You evil monster! I know what you are, you devil, and I curse you! I curse you! You will know this feeling! I promise you, you will know this feeling!'

And as she was shouting, Sir James was shouting too: 'Order! Order! Someone remove this woman from the courtroom!'

And Elizabeth was seized and dragged howling from the room.

Everyone's focus was on the accused and perhaps no one but Alizon saw Jennet's face. Noted her blank, expressionless eyes and a small, secret, curling smile. For the first time Alizon was afraid of her sister. Deathly afraid.

After Elizabeth had left the room, Roger Nowell lifted Jennet onto the stand so that the crowd could see her properly. She looked sweet, so innocent, a poor child caught up in a horrible situation. Roger encouraged her to talk, and Jennet began again.

'I have reason to believe my mother is a witch. I have seen her talk with the Devil. I have seen her familiar.' Here, her eyes wheeled around and met Alizon's. 'A dog. I have witnessed meetings, when my mother has asked for help with murders. I was there during the meeting at Malkin Tower, after my grandmother and sister were arrested. My mother intended to blow up Lancaster Castle using witchcraft, and rescue those locked inside. That was her plan.'

The crowd listened, transfixed. Alizon's feeling of dread deepened.

'You are very brave, young girl.' Sir Edward's patronising voice. 'You have done a good thing here today. You are ridding this world of evil. You may go. Well done.'

Jennet was led from the room, her innocent little head bowed.

'James Device, we call on you as witness.'

Alizon started at the name of her brother. Ginter stepped forward to pull James to the stand. He was shaking, his hair long and wild, his eyes rolling in fear, the front of his breeches stained with what looked like urine.

'You have evidence against your mother?' Sir James asked.

'Yes... yes! I saw her... a victim... John Robinson... he was my friend, I... he, I saw her...'

'I need you to speak clearly.'

James gulped. 'I saw my mother. She made a clay figure. I saw her make a clay figure of John Robinson.'

Alizon looked closely at her brother. He looked broken, wrong. She wondered what he had been through before he agreed to make this statement. This lie.

Sir James nodded, and her brother was dragged back to the bench, breathing quickly and shallowly.

A brief interval while Sir James and Sir Edward muttered between themselves again.

Sir James stood. 'It is clear that Elizabeth Device is a witch. Therefore, we convict her in her absence.'

The despair was all-consuming. Alizon had nowhere to go from here. Her mother was lost, her grandmother was lost, and then…

'James Device.'

James was dragged back to the stand.

'James, you are accused of the murders by witchcraft of Anne Townley and John Duckworth. How do you plead?'

'Not guilty.'

James was gripping the stand tightly, but Alizon could see his legs shaking regardless.

'You are sure?' Sir James asked.

James nodded. Alizon imagined that they had struck a deal. Evidence against her mother, and the charges against him would be dropped. That was surely what had happened.

But then…

'Jennet Device, to the stand please.'

The shaking took over James. Jennet was escorted back to the stand. James did not even look at her. He was shaking his head.

'No. No. No. No no no. No,' he was muttering to himself. 'No no no. No.'

Jennet took her place, and began to talk.

'I have seen my brother summon a large dog.' Her eyes met Alizon's. 'I saw him talk to the dog. He asked the dog to help him kill Anne Townley.' Jennet lowered her gaze.

Sir James nodded again and Jennet was taken away.

'This evidence is clear, James,' he said. He turned to Sir Edward. More whispers. Then:

'James Device. You are convicted of murder by witchcraft. May God take mercy on your soul.'

James collapsed in a howl. He was taken from the room. The whispers of the crowd sounded like a numb buzzing in Alizon's ears. Her grandmother. Her mother. Her brother.

Sir Edward stood. 'We will end today's court session here. We will return tomorrow to try the rest of the accused.'

The court erupted in noise. Talking, the excited shouts of a worked-up crowd. Curious looks at those remaining on the bench. Alizon felt herself lifted; she was being taken away, through the pressing crowd. Back into sunlight. Back down a staircase. Back through a corridor. Back into a cell. Somebody already there.

'Did they get you too?' her mother asked quietly.

Alizon shook her head numbly. 'Not yet. I didn't have my turn.'

'Tomorrow?'

Alizon nodded.

'What happened?'

'James.'

Elizabeth nodded.

They sat silently for some time. Alizon imagined Old Annie and Anne Redferne doing the same in their cell.

'Why did Jennet…?' Alizon asked.

'She is an evil, foul beast and I will hear no more of her. She has seen the way she wants to go, and she has taken it and damned us all.' Elizabeth's face was clenched. Tears came.

19

Touching distance
Almost here
All together
All together

19 AUGUST 1612

No sleep. Just sitting. Silently contemplating. Alizon couldn't bear to think of her turn on the stand. She wondered briefly whether she would deny it all or confess, but her mind shied away. She never wanted tomorrow to come. She wanted tomorrow to come more quickly. She wanted it over. She never wanted it to be over. She wanted it to stop. She wanted it to speed up.

And just like that, too soon, not soon enough, the familiar sound of metal on metal. She was taken alone this time, her mother left in the cell. No cold water today. The guards seemed to be in a rush. Alizon could see from the sun that it was advancing afternoon.

Back into the courtroom. A reduced number of them on the bench today. Sir James, Sir Edward and Roger were already sitting at the table, Thomas Potts fluttering around them like a giant moth.

The crowd swelled as one when Alizon was led through them. An angry, singular body, focusing on her. Alizon was led to the end of the bench, chained up as before.

Sir James stood. He looked tired today, as though his godly task was weighing on him. It was with a grave face that he gazed at the scroll in front of him.

'Anne Redferne. To the stand.'

Anne Redferne stood. Ginter made to grab Anne's arm and drag her, but Anne shook him off and walked steadily and with dignity to the stand.

'Anne Redferne. You are accused of the murder by witchcraft of Christopher Nutter. How do you plead?'

She spoke in a loud voice. Clear as a bell. 'Not guilty.'

A big sigh. 'You are sure that is how you want to plead?'

'Yes. I barely knew Christopher Nutter. I was just a child when he died. This was over thirty years ago, I think? I was a child. All I remember of him was that he was an old, sick man. These accusations are lies.'

She sounded confident. Alizon believed her, fully. The crowd did too. They were nodding. Sir James and Sir Edward were nodding.

The nodding frustrated Roger Nowell. He stood suddenly, remembered himself, sat down again. Leaned over to whisper in Sir James's ear. Sir James looked at him. A long hard look. Then spoke.

'We have evidence from Sheriff Nowell's investigations. Thomas?'

Thomas shuffled through the scrolls, selected one and began to read. Roger Nowell leaned back, his arms folded.

'And on this day Elizabeth Southern came before me. She had a hunched back, and blind in both eyes...'

Roger waved his hand; Thomas nodded nervously and skimmed over the scroll.

'She accused one Anne Redferne of making

clay figures in the shape of Christopher Nutter, then crushing them. Elizabeth Southern confirmed Anne Redferne to be a witch more dangerous than her mother.' Thomas glanced up.

Roger nodded.

Sir James frowned. 'Elizabeth Southern?'

Roger cleared his throat. 'Yes. Mother to Elizabeth Device. Grandmother to James Device, Alizon Device and Jennet Device. Herself accused to be a witch. Died in custody.'

Sir James nodded. 'I see. Is this all of the evidence?'

Roger affirmed.

He sounded unconvinced. Alizon was unconvinced too. She knew she herself had said things against Anne Redferne, but it was clear to her that she had done nothing. There was a long debate between the two Sirs. The crowd were talking too. They sounded just as unconvinced as Alizon.

Time passed.

Sir James stood. 'Anne Redferne. We find you guilty of murder by witchcraft.'

A grumble in the crowd, which grew and grew. They seemed unsatisfied with the verdict. Sir

James shrugged, and Anne visibly shrank as she was led away.

Any small faith that Alizon had had in this trial was gone.

Alizon looked down the bench. There were six of them left. Five women, including her, and a man. She knew all of them by sight, a few by name. Some she knew from the village, some had been treated by her mother. There was the butcher's wife, and the miller's. She had been treated by Elizabeth for a pain in the stomach some years ago. None of them were witches. What were they doing here?

Her question was answered almost immediately.

'We now call Jennet Device back to the stand.'

Jennet was led in. An innocent look on her innocent face.

Sir James looked very serious. His eyes were sharp now. 'Jennet. We have need of your help. A serious matter occurred on 10 April of this year, Good Friday. There was a gathering in your home. Do you remember?'

A small nod.

'This gathering is believed to have been a gathering of witches. We need you to tell us who was there. Can you do it?'

Another small nod.

'Well. Come with me.' Sir James, clearly trying to sound kindly and jovial, stood and walked around the table. He took Jennet's hand.

Even Alizon could see that it lay limp in his.

Sir James took her to the woman sitting on the end of the bench closest to the table.

'Jane Bulcock. Was she at the meeting?'

A dumpy woman who often talked to Elizabeth at the well.

'Oh, yes!' Jennet's sing-song voice. 'I remember. She spoke of how she once killed Jennet Deane.'

Scratching of quills. Eager faces.

'John Bulcock. Was he at the meeting?'

Jane's son. Thick brow, dark eyes.

'Why, yes! He turned the spit, the spit for the sheep my brother James stole! And he spoke of helping his mother with Jennet Deane.'

Gasps. An audible moan from John.

'Alice Nutter. Was she at the meeting?'

Alizon knew her. A rich woman, really. What was she doing here?

'Yes! She came in at the end of the meeting. She seemed desperate to join them all!'

More gasps. No movement from Alice.

'Katherine Hewitt. Was she at the meeting?'

'Oh, yes, I remember her! She said she murdered a child. Anne Foulds.'

More gasps. Sir James looked sickened. Katherine's eyes filled with tears.

'Alice Grey. Was she at the meeting?'

A mousy woman, sitting next to Alizon on the bench.

'Well, I… well, I… I don't recall…'

'You don't recognise the face?' Sir James asked gently.

Jennet shook her head slowly, eyes making contact with Alizon.

'You are sure?' This shout came from the table, from Roger Nowell.

'Yes.' Defiance from Jennet. 'Yes, I am sure.'

Sir James's eyes moved to Alizon, the last person on the bench. 'Thank you, Jennet, for your time. You have been a great help to us all.'

She was led away again, a strange smile on her face. She left behind her a bench of shaking, groaning adults.

Sir James went back to his bench, leaned in for discussion with Sir Edward and Roger. They looked at scrolls, gestured often, spoke loudly at times. Eventually, Sir James stood.

'Jane Bulcock. John Bulcock. Alice Nutter. Katherine Hewitt. You are all found guilty of murder by witchcraft. Take them away.'

Silence, but some racking sobs from John.

'Alice Grey. You are found not guilty. You may leave.'

This was too much for Alice, who collapsed in a dead faint and had to be carried away. Alizon was the only one left on the bench. Murmuring rose in the crowd. Alizon had melted, she felt sure of it. If someone tried to drag her to that stand, she would spread out across the floor and flow away. There was no way she was solid.

Eventually, the crowd silenced. Sir James stood. And he said five echoing words.

'Alizon Device. To the stand.'

Ginter took hold of her chains, pulled her across the floor. She didn't melt, as she had assumed, but her legs didn't work and she stumbled, fell. Had to be lifted. Eventually she was at the stand. Metal on metal. Her chain was locked onto the iron ring.

'Alizon Device. You are accused of causing harm by witchcraft. How do you plead?'

The room closed in on her. She tried to answer, but there was nothing she could say. No words would come. There was nothing inside her. The men were looking at her expectantly, but there was nothing she could do. Nothing she could say. Panic started. She looked around desperately.

Spotted someone. Someone in the crowd. Someone sitting, when everyone else was standing. A silent stare in a sea of bellowing mouths.

The sound of the wooden hammer.

'The defendant has admitted no plea. John Law to the stand,' Sir James shouted.

John Law.

The silent stare was wheeled forward. He was propped up in a wooden chair which his son pushed slowly forward to the stand.

And as she saw him, Alizon felt a crush of guilt, stronger than any she had ever felt before. Her actions had cost this man his freedom to live and work as he chose. Had condemned his son to a life of caring for a disabled father. Had sent Old Demdike straight to Hell. The crushing weight was so strong, and the pain of it forced her to the floor.

She crawled towards John, put her hands on his legs. 'Forgive me, please forgive me,' she sobbed. 'I wish for nothing more than to take it back. Please, forgive me for what I have done.' The words fell over each other. One after the other, on top of the other, but her meaning was clear.

'Alizon Device. You have confessed to causing harm by witchcraft. You are convicted. Your sentence will be death by hanging.'

The sound of the wooden hammer.

She was being taken away, the humming crowd following her. She saw John Law looking at her. A slight nod. That was it. The forgiveness she wanted. She had it. She stored it in her heart. No one could take that. Back into the cell with her mother, who glanced at her face.

'They got you too, then?'

Alizon didn't need to answer.

20

Glory. Triumph.
It is here.
Glory. Triumph.
The time is here.

20 AUGUST 1612

Metal on metal. Too soon. It would always be too soon. There would never be long enough left.

Pulled out. Alizon tried to grab her mother's hand, and was roughly shoved away.

Chains around her wrists.

Pushed forward.

Into sunlight.

A braying crowd.

Slipping on wet, wooden steps.

Bruised knees, pulled upwards.

Facing the crowd.

Mother to her left. Brother to her right. Both shaking, facing the crowd.

Beyond them, others. Old Annie. Anne Redferne. Jane Bulcock. John Bulcock. Alice Nutter. Katherine Hewitt. Facing the crowd, on this wooden ledge.

Legs shaking. Facing the crowd.

There, in the crowd. Was that…?

A hooded man. Executioner. Alighted the steps.

But there, in the crowd, wasn't that…?

The noose. The noose, around her neck.

But there, in the crowd, what was she doing here?

Creaking footsteps from the hooded man.

She was there, it was her, in the crowd. She was watching, waiting.

Creaking, creaking, thumping. Sweat on the forehead.

How had she got there? That blank expression.

Legs giving way. Stumbling up. The man, shouting, reading the list of crimes.

The crowd yelling, but her, standing still. Eyes flashing black.

A knoll. A bell. A lasting ring. One last breath. Then no ground beneath her feet. Falling. Gasping, no air. Gasping. Gasping.

The last sight. Her eyes. It was her. It was her all along.

Jennet.

21

If the well is poisoned
   The well must be filled
   The well must be filled
   Must be filled

1615 – PENDLE

The Tower was razed after the trial, praise the Lord. That evil, stinking place buried beneath the dirt. And they got most of them, didn't they? They got most of them. They just didn't get the worst of them.

    No. She lives on.

Afterword

The 1612 Pendle witch trials were certainly not unique in England at the time, but rather were part of a hunt which led to almost 500 people being executed for the crime of witchcraft after it was made a capital offence in 1563. The last execution for witchcraft in England was in 1684, and laws against the pretence of witchcraft were still in place until the Fraudulent Mediums Act of 1951.

What was unique about the Pendle trials, however, was the weight given to the evidence of a nine-year-old girl for the first time. Prior to this, children under fourteen could not be sworn under oath and were not used as credible witnesses. But the Pendle trials changed all of that.

There are many theories suggesting why Jennet Device gave evidence against her family. Perhaps she truly believed they were witches, perhaps she was clever and wished to be rid of them (as Alizon believes in *The Hellion*), or perhaps, the most likely explanation, Roger Nowell, with his resources and comfortable home, gave Jennet food and shelter and was able to persuade her to say the things she said. The truth of the matter is unknown.

Whether people in the local area were glad that Jennet at least survived or were terrified is also unknown. There are no certain records of her after the trial, no details of where she went, given the deaths of her family and neighbours. Just over twenty years later there was another set of witch trials. This time, the evidence was given by a ten-year-old boy. One of the convicted was a Jennet Device. Was this the same Jennet? Did she meet the same fate as her family? Although there is no record of an execution, there is no record of a release either. The boy eventually admitted to lying, but Jennet was not allowed to leave gaol until she had paid her board for the time spent there. This is likely to have been impossible to achieve.

What we can be certain about is the enormous cultural and religious shift which cumulated in the witch trials. The upheaval in the Church during Henry VIII's reign was the beginning of a cultural sea change which led to Catholicism being seen as superstitious and suspect. For huge swathes of the country, their way of life was thrown into question. Although Whalley Abbey wasn't burnt to the ground and the abbot murdered, as in *The Hellion*, it was dissolved during Henry VIII's sacking of the abbeys and this would have been extremely difficult for the people in the area who often relied on the local religious order in times of hardship.

Given that we have no information about the early lives of Elizabeth Southern and Anne Whittle (Old Demdike and Old Annie), the two matriarchal heads of those families, we cannot know how dissolution affected them. Given their estimated ages at the time of the trials, we can assume that they experienced first-hand much of the upheaval. After early childhoods as Catholics, which was then gradually outlawed as a religion, it is likely that the rituals and routines would have been a source of secret comfort. Whether they then evolved into part of the practices which caused the women to be arrested is debatable, but it is unlikely that the switch to Protestantism would have been accepted and taken up among the residents of Lancashire without any question. It is worth remembering that these people were illiterate – they knew and recognised the incense, confession, prayers and chants. In comparison, the 'new' religion must have felt very odd indeed.

So why did the trials take place? Why was witchcraft so feared? Much of the hysteria can be blamed on King James I, James VI of Scotland, whose book *Daemonologie* – a study of evil – was published in 1597. James was Scottish, and was brought up Protestant, with a fear of evil, witches and Catholics a part of his upbringing. He was ruling over a strange country, and had nearly been killed in the 1605 Gunpowder Plot. He was suspicious of everything, and everyone. This trickled down – ambitious men wishing to gain the approval of the king could do so by unearthing witches. It is clear that Roger Nowell was one such man.

It is interesting how Catholicism and witchcraft became so intrinsically linked in England. In mainland Europe, where Catholicism was the main religion, witch hunts were just as (if not more) popular. James I's fear of witches and the very real possibility that his people were plotting against him had become one. To him, and to England at the time, both Catholics and witches were terrorists and a threat to peace.

The women and men in *The Hellion* existed. Although this is a work of fiction, it is based on a true series of events which are stranger than fairy tales. In 1612, Alizon Device, approximately nineteen years of age, did try to buy some pins from a pedlar. The pedlar refused, so she cursed him. The pedlar dropped to the ground, suffering what is now commonly accepted to have been a stroke. Alizon was gripped by guilt and later confessed. Accounts of her confession suggest that she truly believed her curse had worked, and that she didn't know how to cure him.

Did Alizon experience the internal struggle that I have attributed to her, the difficulty in accepting her family? It is entirely possible, given her confession. She had a strong understanding of what 'witchcraft' could cause, and felt immeasurably guilty for harming a man. We cannot know of the dynamics within the Malkin Tower household, but we can assume it was not always a happy family – particularly given the fact that Jennet was able to criminalise her own mother.

Jennet's father is unknown – she was not the full sibling of Alizon and James, whose father died two years before Jennet was born. Did Alizon believe that she was the daughter of the Devil? It's possible. Based on the customs of the time, we can assume that Jennet attended her family's execution and, if the two did lock eyes, who can imagine what Jennet was thinking?

Alizon, in her confession, named other witches – Old Chattox (Old Annie – Anne Whittle – in *The Hellion*) and Anne Redferne. The court records suggest that there was serious acrimony between the two families. They accused one another of multiple crimes, each member seeming to believe that the worse the accusations against the other family, the lower the likelihood of their own family's conviction. They were wrong.

I have imagined the reasons behind the lack of friendship; there is no record that Old Demdike's husband lived with Anne Whittle, nor that Anne Whittle took the abbot's skull. However, there were whispers of a theft from Anne, and Elizabeth Device believed that Anne cursed her husband, murdering him. It is most likely that both Old Demdike and Anne Whittle were wise women, in rivalry with each other. They probably saw that their only chance for survival lay in blaming the other family, which would also be the perfect way to remove the competition. *The Hellion* puts Anne Whittle as the more successful of the two based on the frequent descriptions of the Device family as beggars and their address – the notorious Malkin Tower.

Malkin Tower has never been found, although there are some theories about the site. It was certainly the venue for the 'meeting of witches', which led to more of those from the local area being executed, thanks to the evidence Jennet gave.

Elizabeth Device, mother of Jennet and Alizon, was described by court documents as being deformed, one eye higher than the other. She was a bright woman, and did not ever confess to the crimes she was accused of. In fact, she was convicted in her absence after Jennet Device was brought into the courtroom. The sight of her daughter caused her to break down and scream in court – she was removed so that Jennet could deliver her evidence.

I have used a little poetic licence in the scenes in Lancaster Gaol. In reality, all of the accused, along with other suspected criminals, were kept in the same small cell. However, as *The Hellion* is about the Southern/Device family, I wanted to stay inside their heads and not spend too long with the other women and men convicted. There are numerous stories that can be told about these other people. There were numerous loves and lives, cut short.

Speaking of loves, we must talk of John Robinson. He was one of the men Anne Whittle was accused of murdering, and although there are no links to Alizon Device, it is not unreasonable to imagine that a nineteen-year-old girl would have experienced love in the previous few years, however short lived. Using John in this way, we are able to see how cut off and lonely the Device way of life must have been.

The biggest question – did they really believe they were witches? The answer is probably yes. Alizon certainly believed in her powers, and it is unlikely that she was the sole practitioner in her family. As has been said, Old Demdike and Anne Whittle were wise women, dabbling in healing and other skills, depending on the price. Until the trials, this would have been a sensible occupation for a widow – a way to keep alive. But, as has been seen countless times throughout history, a woman able to support herself used to attract suspicion.

It would not do to forget the men of the witch trials. James Device is, of course, the one who features most here, but John Bulcock was also executed following the Pendle witch trials. It is estimated that up to 25 per cent of those accused of witchcraft in England were men – overseas, this could be much higher (in Moscow, male witches outnumbered female witches significantly). It is a common misconception that witches were only women. The truth is, anyone could be a witch, with the right person accusing you. The picture of an old woman, crooked nose, cat by her side is more modern than the trials.

Now a moment to write an ode to Pendle, and in particular Pendle Hill. If you have the opportunity to visit, I highly recommend it. As you tramp through the area, the sky likely a leaden grey above you (it is Lancashire, after all), you may feel as though you are travelling back in time. It seems as though very little has changed since those days; the dark wedge of Pendle Hill casting a shadow over the nearby villages. Of course, there are fewer trees – the woods creeping up the hill have become farmland – but the silence is still there. You can see how James I and his loyal men could have been afraid of the area, miles away (not only in distance) from the considerably more metropolitan London.

So, was Jennet a hellion – a rowdy or mischievous child? Probably, given her upbringing. Was she an evil witch, led by the Devil? Those who accused her during her own trial, many years later, would say yes – but I will let you decide.

I have mentioned Jennet's own trial. Although it is not known whether the Jennet Device convicted at a trial which occurred twenty-two years later in 1634 is the same Jennet, it is true that the trial was based on the evidence of a ten-year-old boy, Edmund Robinson. A boy who, when asked by his parents why he was late home, gave an incredible account of greyhounds turning into people, a witches' hall with food falling from the ceiling, and a boy with cloven hooves. Fortunately, times had changed and the evidence was met with far more questions than at the Pendle witch trials.

If only this was the end of it. The precedent of using children's testimony in a witch trial was written in a book for lawmakers, *The Wonderfull Discoverie of Witches in the Countie of Lancaster* by Thomas Potts. That book found its way overseas. Overseas to the colonies. Where a Justice used its words to use the evidence of children in the most notorious of witch trials – in Salem, Massachusetts.

Acknowledgements

None of this would have been done without the unending and loving support of my husband, Michael. It is my dream to one day believe in myself as much as you believe in me. It's cliché to say that you are my rock, but you truly are – and your incredible example of pure discipline has ensured that this book actually got written!

To everyone at Unbound, thank you for all of your hard work and passion in making this dream come true. From cover design to editing, the process has been truly enjoyable thanks to you, and I feel very lucky to work with such a talented team.

I also need to shout an enormous thank you to 'The Unit'. Knowing I have the backing of such a loyal bunch who are always happy to drink gin (preferably

Henstone) with me and listen to me ramble is amazing.

A separate thank you needs to go to my mum and dad. For your constant love and support, no matter what.

To all of my other family and friends, old and new, who have offered advice, love and just been there – thank you. To my wonderful friends on Instagram and the #bookstagram community, know that you are all awesome and this may never have happened without you.

I must end by thanking the following, and assuring them that they (and their suffering) are not forgotten:

Elizabeth Southern (died before trial)

Elizabeth Device (executed)

Alizon Device (executed)

James Device (executed)

Anne Whittle (executed)

Anne Redferne (executed)

Jane Bulcock (executed)

John Bulcock (executed)

Alice Nutter (executed)

Katherine Hewitt (executed)

Alice Grey (found innocent)

Jennet Preston (executed)

And to all of the other victims of a fearful and patriarchal law, both in Britain and overseas.

Unbound Supporters

Unbound is the world's first crowdfunding publisher, established in 2011.

We believe that wonderful things can happen when you clear a path for people who share a passion. That's why we've built a platform that brings together readers and authors to crowdfund books they believe in – and give fresh ideas that don't fit the traditional mould the chance they deserve.

This book is in your hands because readers made it possible. Everyone who pledged their support is listed at the front of the book and below. Join them by visiting unbound.com and supporting a book today.

Martha Adam-Bushell   Claire Adams

Jo Aitken
Ashley Allen
Brittany Arthur
Megan Artz
Athena's Choice
James Aylett
Roberta Azzopardi
Alex Baird
Lorrie Baladad
Sam Ballagh
Joneil Bantolina
Sally Barnes
Joe Barnfather
Alan Barr
Emma Bayliss
Samantha Beard
Louise Beckett
Katinka Behrendt
Leah Bergen
Dawn Blackburn
Cecile Bouteca
Evelyn Braybrooke
Sarah Brousseau
Charlene Brown
Emily Brown
David Brownstein
Claire Burton
Emily Bye
Harriet Rose Bywater
Amber Carnegie
J Carole
Emma Carr
Jonathan Carr
Jacqui Castle
Beth Chown
Alice Clurow
Mindy Collins
Nadine Collins
Tim Condon
Jay Connor
Angela Cotter
Alasdair Coutts-Britton

Sue Crabtree
Karrah Creamer
Helen Crooke
Jessica Currie
George Davin
Brittany Davis
Jacquie Davis
Jourden Davis
Grace Dawson
Kirsty Dawson
Chloé Delforge
Karina Dewi
Taylor Dinkins
Shannon Donaghy
Harriet Dorman
Siobhan Dowd
Lauren Drake
Jenny DuRoss
Charles Edwards
Kate Ellis
Paige Ellis
Raisa Bianca Espeño-Calida
Amy Evans
Janie Evans
Tim Ewins
Anne Feltz
Crow Ferguson
Kate Fletcher
Laura Fontana
Carmen Forján
Julie Gallagher
Anna Gheorghiu
Victoria Gilbert
Liz Gladden
Noella Glasson
Christine Grass
Amanda Gray Williams
Alexandra Greaves
Joanne Green
Rachel Green
Sarah Grotenhuis
Chris Harding

April Hargreaves
Pete Harris
Paula Hartharn-Evans
Anna Hauldren
Abbey Heffer
Jamie Henderson
Claire Hewson
Erin Hiatt
Peter & Heather Hodgson
Lisa Hodson
Amber Hubley
Victoria Huggins
Joe Hurley
Lori Hyett
Michelle Ilardi
Ova Incekaraoglu
Rahayu J
Maya Jacklin
Harriet Jackman
Angela James
Kathryn Jenkinson
Sofia Karakosta
Etta Kavanagh
Heather Kelly
Dan Kieran
Kayla King
Kerry Kissinger
Steph Knight
Denise Köllen
Julia Lackermayer
Aniket Latpate
Katie Lavie
Julie Lawler
Harriet Lawrence
Tim Lee
Angela Leis
Nicole Leonard
Maren Letemple
Lisa Levine
Anastasia Lewis
Joe Lomeli
VJ Lonsdale

Rachel Luney
Lauren Macdonald-Herde
Chloe Macmillan
Dan Madden
Michael Maddison
Bailey Magrann-Wells
Gemma Maguire
Philippa Manasseh
Aishwarya Manohar
Samala Marshall
Katie Martin
David Matthews
Holly McCann
Catherine McClay
Catherine McCollum
Megan McCormick
Erin McDonald
Marie McGinley
Nicola McLean
Chrissy McMorris
Samantha Merritt
Harriet Mills
John Mitchinson
Yelda Moers
Farhiya Mohamed
Willow Moon
Kailie Moroney
Ina Muenster
Lauren Murase
Kirstie Myers
Rhel ná DecVandé
Debbie Nairn
Carlo Navato
Jen Neil
Heather Nelson
Kaitlin Newman
Andra Nicoara
Martin Nolan
Hannah O'keefe
Maria Ortega
Gemma Owen-Kendall
Tope Owolabi

Camilla Marie Pallesen
Kelsey Palmer
Monica Palmer
Aayushi Pandey
Avril Parker-Jones
Thelma Parker-Shimell
Alison Parr
Oliver Pearce
Esme Pears
Emma Pearson
Christopher Pennington
Jack Phillips
Michael Pilgrim
Justin Pollard
Anne-Kathrine Porsbøl
Jessica Pouch
Helen Pratt
Josie Price
Megan Prince
Trevor Prinn
Carl Proffit
Shelby Pumphrey
Jeana Quigley
Jo Race
Aaliyah Rafeeq
Nadia Rahman
Ellie Rayner
Lydia Reaves
Melanie Reid
Iola Reneau
Alejandra Reneses
Anna Richardson
Miranda Rijks
Nicola Rimmer
Charlotte Roberts
Sharon Roberts
Jess Robertson
Martha Rogers
Amanda Rose
Jamie Rose
Nicole Rosito
Leslie Roskam

Vanessa Rubenser
Rafif Ruhaimi
Emily Rushforth
Hannah Ryan
Yousra Samir
Ana Sanjosé Pérez
Charles Sargeant
Kaitlyn Schnobrich
Shelby Schwede
George Peter Martyr Scott
Zeynep Sertkaya
Laura Severn
Ana Shamsi
Divyansh Sharma
Raghav Sharma
Jen Sherman
Mariana Silva
Whitney Simonsen
Alan Sims
Rachel Slocombe
Ella Smith
Hayley Smith
Megan Snell
Sarah Snell
Hayley Solano
Thania Solar
Katherine Sopova
Karen Southcote-Want
Jess Spataro
Richard Spencer
Lycka Ståhl
Johanna Stapleton
Jessica Stefani
Sophia Sternmeer
Rosalyn Stewart
Armelle Steyaert
Mark Strongman
Nina Stutler
Anna Szepietowska
Georgette Taylor
Pam Taylor
Sarah Taylor

Rebekah Thomas
Tracey Thompson
Catherine Thorn
Cheyenne Thornton
Lynne Threlfall
David Toller
Imogen Toller
Steve Toller
Rafe Toller-Blackburn
Kim Tornberg
Dana Tors
Christopher Trent
Aleksander Trøen
Debbie Turner
Katerina Turner
Ljiljana Udovicic
Marina Uzunova
Sonja van Amelsfort
Abigail Walker
Angela Wallace
Jessica Warr

Chris Watts
Dennis Whitehead
Carys Wiggans
Indra Wignall
Katie Wilcox
Bev and Vaughan Wilkinson
Huw Williams
Jenny Williams
Maureen Williams
Sophia Williams
Alexis Willis
Derek Wilson
Misty Wilson
Zoe Wotzko
Gina Yacub
Christine, Priya, Fifi, Scott, Ritchie, Kitchen Young
Ana Zapata
Crystal Zavala
Lucy Zeitlin